THE TROUBLE WITH
Miss Switch

Barbara Brooks Wallace

ALADDIN PAPERBACKS
New York London Toronto Sydney Singapore

For Jimmy of Clan Wallace
with love and the usual

First Aladdin Paperbacks edition June 2002
Text copyright © 1971 by Barbara Brooks Wallace

ALADDIN PAPERBACKS
An imprint of Simon & Schuster
Children's Publishing Division
1230 Avenue of the Americas
New York, NY 10020

Design by Ann Sullivan
The text of this book was set in Berkeley Oldstyle ITC.
Printed in the United States of America
2 4 6 8 10 9 7 5 3

Cataloging-in-Publication Data available from
the Library of Congress.

ISBN 0-689-85177-4

CONTENTS

Rupert P. Brown III, Scientist

It was in the summer following my year in the fourth grade that I, Rupert P. Brown III, became a great scientist. As a scientist, I feel I must make the following report of the strange events that took place upon my entering the fifth grade.

You could tell by my room that summer what a great scientist I'd become. Take, for instance, the pile of things on my desk. There were a lot of nails (rusty but still useful), three magnets, some pieces of broken pop bottle, half of a pair of scissors, seven and one-half inches of a plastic ruler, a mag-

1

nifying glass, a piece of copper coil, and a wad of green and red rubber bands. That was just the top layer. There were a lot more useful things below it. To make sure that nobody (like my mother, for instance) monkeyed around trying to straighten things out, I had a warning on my desk written with white chalk on a black piece of paper—"ANYONE WHO REMOVES WILL BE PERSECUTED—SIGNED, THE LAW!" I had also drawn a skull and crossbones just for insurance.

Of course, I had a microscope. It was on the bookcase with my eggshell collection, which I kept on a bed of cotton in an old sneaker box. I labeled, and took notes on, everything. My eggshells were "white breasted nuthatch," "golden crowned kinglet," "yellow billed cuckoo," "chicken," and "duck."

I had five mason jars filled with water, floating greenery, and snails, which I labeled "aquarium experiment." Also another jar holding my mildewed orange, which I labeled "mold experiment." Besides this, there was my live turtle, labeled "Caruso—turtle experiment" (which was cheating because I wasn't experimenting anything with him, he was just my pet), and my two guinea pigs (one thin and starved looking and the other one overstuffed), which I labeled "Hector and Guinevere—nutrition experiment."

Besides all this, there was my rock collection, my leaf collection, my shell collection, my beetle collection, and my butterfly collection. You can understand why I wasn't anxious to leave all this behind just to enter the fifth grade.

I've never looked forward to the first day of school, anyway. My theory is that it should be abolished. The trouble is that the second day of school would then become the first day, and you'd be right back where you started. Kids are stuck with it any way you look at it. My second theory is, however, that you should let your parents know how you feel about it so they'll suffer and feel guilty. Unfortunately, this second theory doesn't work too well either. You can be bleeding to death on the first day of school, but you go to school, bleeding or no bleeding.

"Rupert!"

That was my name being called musically from the kitchen on the morning of my first day in the fifth grade. I have to hand it to my mother. She always tries to make the first day of school as pleasant as possible even though it's *impossible*.

The lump under the blanket on my bed, which happened to be me, shifted slightly.

"Rupert!"

I opened my eyes cautiously and saw that the sunlight was coming through an assortment of holes in the window shade where I'd shot some home-made arrows a few weeks before. I was also an amateur Indian that summer besides being a great scientist. Then I threw back my covers, put one leg over to see if the floor was still there, and waited for the smell of cinnamon toast to come drifting up the stairs. Naturally there would be cinnamon toast for breakfast. It was one of my favorite foods, and I knew that my mother would do everything to dull the pain, preparing my favorite breakfast and all that. I could have told her that she was wasting her time, because I knew that I'd hardly touch anything.

"Rupert!"

My mother never gives up. I shot myself in and out of the clothes closet in three seconds, took another fifteen seconds to dress, grabbed my glass-es from the desk, and polished them on my trousers as I sauntered down the stairs. I'd forgot-ten to put on my shoes, but my mother seemed to know I was coming anyway.

"Rupert, have you brushed your teeth?" she called through the dining room from the kitchen.

"Yes," I said.

"Did you brush them thoroughly?"

"Yes!" I shouted, coming through the kitchen door.

My father looked up from the morning newspaper. "What your mother means is did you brush your teeth *this* morning?"

"Oh," I said, turning and going back out the door. I forgot about my teeth on the way to the bathroom, but when I stopped to feed my fat guinea pig, Guinevere, her nutritionally balanced diet, I did remember something else.

"Where are they?" I shouted down the stairs.

My father replied, "Did you try your mouth? They were there last night!" My father thinks he's very funny.

"I meant my sneakers!" I shouted.

"Oh!" my father shouted back.

"Try the bookshelf, dear!" shouted my mother.

I did, and found my sneakers on top of my book *Science for the Intermediate Scientist,* which I thumbed through before heading back downstairs.

"And how is The Law this morning?" asked my

father. His voice sounded hollow coming from behind an extra-large coffee cup marked TO FATHER in red nail polish. I'd done that in kindergarten where I became a great artist.

I threw myself down at the table. "*Very* funny!" I said. "I'm miserable, if you really care to know."

"I wouldn't have asked if I didn't," said my father.

"Never mind, dear," said my mother, putting down in front of me a glass of milk, a glass of orange juice, a plate on which were two fried eggs surrounded by six slices of bacon, and a smaller plate which had on it a neat stack of three pieces of cinnamon toast. "Eat your breakfast and you'll feel better."

I gazed off into space. "I told you I didn't think I'd be able to eat," I said.

"Well, do the best you can," said my mother. She turned back to the stove and put two more slices of cinnamon toast under the broiler.

"Cheer up, old man," said my father. I caught him looking at me over the top of his paper and quickly put down the slice of toast I was biting into. "You know," he went on, "the first day of school isn't the worst thing that can happen to you. You've lived through two or three that I can remember."

"The only thing worse than the first day of school is the first day of school *next* year," I said as I forced down the last of my first egg. "And anyway, who's going to look after all my experiments while I'm gone all day?" I choked down the remainder of my orange juice.

"I'm sure the guinea pigs will survive. You're starving Hector anyway, and Guinevere has enough lard around her middle to carry her across the Sahara Desert without another meal. And as for the orange . . . I'm sure it will rot away happily without anyone to mother it for a few hours."

"I hope so," I said. "I can't let school interfere with the progress of science."

"Well, I'm sure the school doesn't want to," said my father. "Anyway, I'm glad to see that you managed to swallow a little breakfast," he said, looking at my empty milk glass, empty orange juice glass, and two empty plates. I ignored this funny remark.

"Won't you have another slice of toast?" my mother asked, pulling the pan from the broiler.

I was busy thinking, so when she put the piece

of toast on my plate, I picked it up and began to munch it without noticing. "I'm not very hungry," I said, "but I guess I will."

"Will what?" asked my mother.

"Have another piece of toast," I said.

"Oh," said my mother, and put the last piece on my plate.

"Attaboy!" said my father, rising from the table. "The sun will shine again. Things will look brighter tomorrow. I wish I could be entering the fifth grade again!" He walked out the door whistling.

Ha! I could be cheerful about it too if I was in my father's shoes.

School! Aw phooey!

I sighed, rose gloomily from the table, and went over to the counter to see if I could find a crumb or two to fill the empty spots in my stomach.

2

Miss Switch

"Hi, Broomstick!" someone said, coming up and almost knocking me over with a slap on the back. I was standing in front of Peppy P. S., otherwise known as Pepperdine Public School.

"Hi!" I said, giving a cough to indicate that I was choking to death.

That was one good thing about the first day of school, anyway—seeing all the gang again.

"Hi, Banana!"

"Hi, Peatmouse!"

"Hi, Creampuff!"

Hardly anybody went by their right names anymore. Banana was Harvey Fanna. Peatmouse was Wayne Partlow. Creampuff was Tommy Conrad. Broomstick, of course, was me, Rupert P. Brown III. I thought the name was fine, since I *am* pretty long and skinny. But any name was fine as long as they forgot the P. in the middle. That was the dark secret of the ages.

The last bell rang, and Banana, Peatmouse, Creampuff, and I filed in, pushing, shoving, and tripping each other all the way to the classroom. It was so pleasant that I almost forgot where I was. But not quite. I was reminded by the weird hollow sounds in the school hall, and by the old, familiar, combined smells of wax on the linoleum, disinfectant on the walls, and soup being boiled in the cafeteria. I sighed and shoved Banana and Creampuff with my elbow.

The class pushed into Room Twenty and found desks for themselves. I had my first chance to look around the classroom. Besides my pals and my archenemy, Amelia Daley, there were some other people I'd known before. Unfortunately, one of them was Melvin Bothwick. Why did we have to have *him* again? I asked myself. It's all right to have

10

a brain, but a sneaky brain is something else. Billy Swanson was there, too. I wasn't exactly thrilled about that either. Billy was a big bully. Still, he could make life interesting for the teacher, which made life interesting for us.

I had talked over in detail the possibility of having a decent teacher this year with my above-mentioned archenemy, Amelia. We had discussed it all the way to school, or at least until the school came into sight. Then we'd parted company without a word when I slowed down to a crawl so that Amelia could move ahead. I wouldn't be seen dead walking to school with a girl, and I considered Amelia a big snoop anyway. The only reason I walked with her at all was because we'd been walking to school together since we were in the first grade and I didn't know a good way to get out of it.

Anyway, when I entered the classroom, I took a long, hard look at my fifth grade teacher. Then I took off my glasses, put them back on, and looked again. The teacher, who was sitting at her desk, was busy reading a book and paying no attention to the class at all. I thought this was pretty peculiar. But what I thought even more peculiar was her appearance.

She was wearing a very old-fashioned-looking

dress, really ancient. It was made of some sort of dull gray material. The collar of the dress went up high around her neck and was edged in something white. I think my mother would call it a pleated ruffle. Her black hair was pulled back from her face and rolled up in a kind of bun which sat on her neck. Her neck was thin and her face long, ending in a pointed chin. Her skin was very white, like library paste. On her nose, which was sharp and pinched, there sat a pair of metal-framed spectacles which looked like some kind of gray grasshopper (*genus chelimum,* I told myself) perching on a thin reed. The teacher's whole appearance was about as uncomfortable looking as a steel knitting needle. I shuddered.

The teacher's eyes were turned down to her book and I couldn't see them. But at the very moment when the scuffling and shuffling of everyone finding desks was over, and we all sat there uncomfortable and silent, the teacher looked up.

I've never seen anybody's eyes doing what her eyes were doing. They actually crackled. I could almost see real sparks fly out from them. How could I continue being miserable with this unusual scientific phenomenon going on right in front of me? I wiped my glasses again and stared determinedly at the teacher.

"I am going to ask each one of you his name," she said, "and then I shall write it on the board. That way I shall get to know you more quickly, and you will get to know each other."

She rose, and turned to face the board as everyone in the class looked at each other. As she rose, her skirts made a strange swishing sound.

"Seat one, row one," the teacher called out. "Please begin."

"Bothwick, Melvin J.," said Melvin Bothwick, looking very pleased with himself.

"And what does the J. stand for?" asked the teacher. My heart sank. What difference did it make what the J. stood for?

"James," answered Melvin.

"Next," said the teacher. I noticed how sharp her voice was. It was like the rest of her. It cut through the classroom like the sound of icicles snapping on a thin, frosty morning.

"Fanna, Harvey Robert," said Harvey Fanna.

"Daley, Amelia Matilda," said Amelia Daley.

"Conrad, Tommy No Middle Name," said Tommy Conrad.

My spirits rose considerably. That was exactly

the answer I'd give—No Middle Name. I shot a grateful look at Conrad, Tommy No Middle Name.

"Next!" came the sharp request.

I looked around the room, shined my thumbnail on my shirt a few times, and said very carefully, "Brown, Rupert No Middle Name."

"That won't do!" snapped the teacher. "Can't you give me the correct middle name?"

I was dumbfounded. How had she guessed? "Well, it's . . . that's . . . impossible!" I stammered.

"Rupert Impossible Brown!" wrote the teacher on the blackboard. Then, without looking around she said, "Yes, Melvin?" Melvin had raised his hand.

"Rupert's real middle name is Peevely," said Melvin, looking around the class with a big smug look on his face. "I saw it in the front office registration chart." I think he expected the class to cheer, but no one did.

"I don't like tattletales," said the teacher briskly, still without turning around. "You will write 'My name is Melvin Tattletale Bothwick' one hundred times starting right now. Next!"

My terrible secret was out, but it didn't seem to bother me too much. For one thing, I knew the class was on my side and not Melvin's, and they probably wouldn't mention the Peevely matter again. And for another, I was too puzzled about the teacher to worry further about it. I was positive that the teacher hadn't turned around and seen Melvin's hand go up. I'd heard of people having eyes in the back of their heads, but that was just something you said. I'd certainly never heard of anyone proving it scientifically.

I was still thinking all this over when I saw Billy Swanson carefully and quietly draw a drinking straw from his lunch bucket, tear a little piece of paper from a sandwich wrapping, put it in his mouth, and begin to chew. I knew exactly what was going to happen because I'd seen Billy do this a large number of times in the past. When he had chewed the piece of paper enough to satisfy himself, he pulled it from his mouth and inserted it into the straw. Then he put the straw in his mouth and blew. The whole class, including me, gasped as the spitball struck the teacher right in the middle of her back and bounced onto her desk.

"You may rise, William Robert Swanson," said the teacher, still without looking around. William Robert Swanson rose.

"Next," called the teacher.

She continued to call off names, and William Robert Swanson continued to stand. He looked more uncomfortable every minute.

The whole class was watching the great spectacle of Billy Swanson being uncomfortable in the middle of the classroom. The whole class, that is, except me. I was staring at the teacher's back and at the spitball lying on her desk.

Suddenly I saw the craziest thing happen. I saw the spitball rise up from the teacher's desk.

It rose up and up for several inches (I estimated about a foot and two inches actually), stopped as if to take aim, and then flew with the force of a hailstone right up to William Robert Swanson's cheek, where it landed with a dull smack and fell to his desk. The teacher had never turned around—once!

"Someone hit me with a spitball!" roared Billy.

"You are absolutely right! *I* did!" said the teacher, whirling around. Her eyes crackled like a furnace.

Billy's face turned as red and lumpy as a cherry pie. He shifted miserably from one foot to the other and looked as if he were going to cry.

"May I sit down?" he asked in a meek voice.

"Naturally," said the teacher. "Next!"

When all the names had been called out, the teacher once again turned and faced the class. "Now," she said, "there might be some of you who will need to know who I am from time to time. Therefore, I shall write my name on the board, too." With that she turned and, as if her hand were a bird flying over the blackboard, she wrote in big swooping letters:

MISS SWITCH

The class studied the name closely, and I studied it *very* closely.

"Are there any questions?" Miss Switch asked. There seemed to be no questions except mine, and I kept *those* to myself.

Books were passed out. Lessons were assigned. And the day passed without further excitement other than my friend H. Banana sitting on his chewing gum, and my friend W. Peatmouse chewing the eraser off his pencil and accidentally swallowing it.

But when I returned home that afternoon, I raced up to my room, pulled out a small notebook from my desk, and on the first page of it wrote,

"Miss Switch—Notes." On the next page I wrote:

What: Eyes
Kind: Crackling
Whose: Hers
Performance: Sees clearly from back of head
How Tested: No known way to prove scientifically

And on the next page after that I wrote:

What: Ball
Kind: Spit
Whose: William Robert Swanson's
Performance: Flew without visible means of
    projection
How Tested: No known way to prove scientifically

Then I hid the notebook in my drawer marked "Private—Keep Out—This Means You!" and went to feed Guinevere.

Further Observations

And that was the way it all began. As the days grew shorter, and the nights grew colder, and the leaves on the trees turned from green to bright red and gold, my notebook became filled with information which there was "no known way to prove scientifically."

I managed somehow to restrain myself from revealing my observations and deductions to Banana, Peatmouse, Creampuff, or anyone else. After all, as I told myself, they might stare or gawk or gasp at the wrong moment and ruin the whole thing. As a scientist in search of the truth, I couldn't afford to take this chance. I supposed it was probably my interest in science developing keen powers of observation that had caused me to see all this where it had escaped the others. No, I repeated to myself, I couldn't take the chance of ruining everything by blabbing to someone.

One person, however, worried me. That was Amelia Daley. I could never be sure about Amelia. She certainly wasn't a scientist, but she was a terrible snoop.

"I like Miss Switch," Amelia said to me as we walked to school one day. "The whole class likes Miss Switch."

I thought that remark over very carefully, wondering whether I should or should not consider it a snoopy kind of thing to say before I replied carefully, "Oh, she's all right."

"Well, she makes things interesting, anyway," Amelia said, looking at me sideways.

"I guess so," I said, looking straight ahead. Amelia certainly was wasting her time trying to get anything out of *me,* I thought. By then it was time for me to slow down to a crawl so that Amelia could move on ahead, and the conversation ended. I continued, however, to think over what Amelia had just said.

She was right. I couldn't deny it. Miss Switch really made things interesting. Amelia was also right about the whole class liking her. Especially the boys, I added to myself. I tried to figure out why. Maybe it was because Miss Switch was so fair. When she was nasty, she was nasty to everyone, even the girls. And when she was nice, she was nice to everyone, even the boys. She never wrote on a boy's paper that it would have been an A except that she couldn't read the handwriting. And she even went so far as to have mostly boys on the committee to write the play we were going to put on, which has never been heard of in the whole history of Pepperdine. Therefore we won't be doing some dumb thing with fairies and princes and love and all that other stuff. No wonder the boys liked her. They liked her so much they even went so far as to worry about the way she looked, a subject previously reserved by the girls.

"I think she should undo the bun and let her hair just hang around," said Banana.

"Yeah, like that lady that rode around on the horse in England . . . you know . . . Lady Godzilla," said Creampuff.

"I think that was Godiva," said Peatmouse. "And besides, I don't think the school would like it."

"Why not?" asked Creampuff.

"Because then she couldn't see anything, dummy," said Peatmouse.

"Well, I think she should keep it the way it is. It balances her head scientifically," I said. The others all looked bored at this remark.

Anyway, that's what made it all so difficult—liking Miss Switch. As a scientist, I couldn't let my consideration of Miss Switch as a teacher affect my consideration of her as *something else*. I had to continue observing the unusual phenomena that went on in the classroom and form my conclusions.

Take, for instance, the following event.

One day H. Banana raised his hand and asked to be excused for a drink of water. It's practically a scientific fact that when one person in the class becomes thirsty, so does everyone else. Half the class then raised their hands.

"All right," said Miss Switch, "we will all file out at the same time."

Everyone in the class looked at each other. Usually we went in pairs, and this made getting a drink of water like a kind of miniature recess. The object was to see how long you could make it last before someone was sent out to see if you had drowned in the water fountain.

At any rate, the class all stood up, formed a line at the door, and shoved its way through. Melvin Bothwick stood next in line behind Banana. Right after Banana had had his drink, Melvin put his head down. The class waited. Melvin's head stayed down. The water kept bubbling into Melvin's face. The water bubbled and bubbled and still Melvin kept his face down. The class grew anxious.

"Help!" gurgled Melvin. "I'm drowning. I'm filled with water. I can't lift up my head. I can't turn off the water. Help!"

The class looked as if it expected Miss Switch to throw Melvin a life preserver, but Miss Switch just stood there with her arms folded and said, "Who would like to take Melvin's place?"

No one volunteered.

Finally Peatmouse raised his hand.

"Are you volunteering?" Miss Switch asked.

"No, Miss Switch," said Peatmouse. "I think I'd

like to go back to the room. I'm not thirsty anymore."

The rest of the class suddenly decided it wasn't thirsty either, so we all went back to the room, filing and not shoving. The water stopped bubbling and Melvin was able to raise his head and join us. But as I passed the water fountain, I stuck out my hand and gave the handle a quick turn. The water rose and fell just as it had always done through first, second, third, and fourth grades. My notes that evening read:

What: Fountain
Kind: Water
Whose: Pepperdine Public School's
Performance: Stayed on through remote control
How Tested: No known way to prove scientifically

After I had made the notes, I began to doodle on a piece of notebook paper, and when I'd finished, I sat for a long time and stared at what I'd written:

Miss Switch
Miss (S)witch
Miss Witch

4

Witchcraft Research

Could Miss Switch be only an accident of science—like the time before I'd become a nutritional expert, when I'd fed my old white rat a diet of toothpaste and it had lived (for a while anyway)? No, I reasoned, Miss Switch was no accident of any kind. She was real. She was as real as I was. Except that I was an ordinary human person, and she was—A WITCH!

But she couldn't be! There was no such thing as a witch, and there was no such thing as witchcraft either. If there were, you ought to be able to prove it scientifically, and I couldn't prove one thing about Miss Switch or the things she did. And yet, though I couldn't actually prove anything, wasn't it my powers of observation that had led me to finding out Miss Switch's true nature? I couldn't deny it.

In the end, I could only admit that there was such a thing as witchcraft, because my keen scientific eyes would never deceive me, and what I'd been seeing was witchcraft, real witchcraft. And my keen scientific brain reasoned that, therefore, Miss Switch had to be a witch.

The question was, what was I going to do about it? Did I need to do anything? After all, what had Miss Switch done that was so wrong anyway? She'd just been the neatest teacher we boys had ever had, that's all.

And what if I did report Miss Switch to the authorities (that would be Mr. Denton, the principal)? Heck! When I tried to explain my notes about a nervous water faucet or a flying spitball, he'd probably tell me to go out and get my glasses checked.

But supposing, just *suppposing,* he got nosy. Something might happen to Miss Switch and there would go the greatest opportunities for scientific observation of nonscientific phenomena ever granted anyone in the whole world.

There was one thing that worried me, though, a *big* thing. Miss Switch hadn't done anything really wicked—so far! But I'd heard a few things about witches, and it was what she could and might do that scared me. What could I do about that short of reporting her? What could I do, I finally decided, was present the problem to her *personally*. I could advise her in a very nice way that she was being observed and to just please watch herself.

After all, I reminded myself, as a scientist I should certainly look at all sides of a question, and I hadn't looked at anything from Miss Switch's point of view. Supposing she had a good explanation of herself. Would it be fair to report her to someone (even if they didn't believe me) without talking to her first? And speaking of "fair," that was another thing. How could I be unfair to the fairest teacher I knew? And wasn't it Miss Switch the teacher I was dealing with as well as Miss Switch the witch? Yes, the first person I should discuss the problem with was definitely Miss Switch.

There *was* one other thing, and I think I should mention it. That was the possibility that I COULD

BE WRONG. As a scientist, I feel that I must disclose this other minor reason that led me to my decision to see Miss Switch first.

That evening I decided, however, that before approaching Miss Switch, I'd need much more information than just what I'd learned from my notes, and the place to get that would be the public library. I'd go there the very next day, and after that, depending on what additional facts I learned, I'd arrange to have a private meeting with Miss Switch.

I could hardly keep my mind on school the next day despite the fact that as a scientist in search of the truth, I knew I shouldn't overlook any opportunity of observing *anything*. Until lunch period that day, however, the only observation I made was that the oatmeal I'd had for breakfast didn't last too well, and I was almost dead from starvation by the time the noon bell rang. I considered asking someone to carry me to the cafeteria. Unfortunately, my friends had practically died from starvation too, so Banana, Creampuff, Peatmouse, and I ended up leaning on each other and gasping and choking all the way to the lunch table.

After lunch I wasn't too alert, having helped myself to three ice cream cups, but I did manage to note that when Creampuff and Banana leaned over to pick up a piece of paper for the purpose of carrying on an under-the-desk committee meeting, they found themselves unable to rise for some time. By the time they did, both suffered from stiff necks for the rest of the afternoon.

Outside of that, and observing again the way in which Miss Switch erased the blackboard (only one good swish to make a whole blackboard full of writing disappear), nothing much interesting happened.

It wasn't a completely wasted day, however. While I was busy dozing at my desk, I was also rehearsing the conversation I intended to have with Miss Switch.

I saw myself standing by her desk in the nice, friendly classroom one afternoon after school. The sun would be shining through the windows, warming up our jars of indoor gardens and lighting up the corkboard that held the curled-up sheets of paper (one of them mine) that were the class's best work.

I would listen to the small scratching sounds of

Pepe (for Pepperdine), the class mascot, whirling around on his wire wheel. I would draw a deep breath, taking in the encouraging smells of chalk dust, book bindings, and an old peanut butter sandwich that Peatmouse had kicked under my desk five days before.

Then I'd bow low from the waist in a gentlemanly manner and say, "Miss Switch, I want you to know what a neat teacher we boys think you are." I'd pause here while Miss Switch told me how pleased she was. Then I'd continue. "There's just one little thing, though, that's been bothering me. It's nothing much, really, but being a gentleman, I thought I ought to discuss it with you before I discussed it with anyone else." I thought I might just bow again here. "The point is, Miss Switch . . ."

I never did get to the point because at that moment the closing bell rang. It didn't matter. I knew that I'd have plenty of time to rehearse my speech later. I had no intention of talking to Miss Switch until I was *ready*. So, on to the library and then on to see Miss Switch.

No, not quite on to see Miss Switch. There was one more thing I wanted to do first, and I was going to do it that night! My insides quaked at the thought. But I considered the scientists who went into steamy jungles filled with poisonous plants and insects, or climbed the sheer sides of icy, jagged mountains in their quest for knowledge. Going out into the dark, fearsome night to do what I was going to do was a small price to pay for scientific truth. I'd made up my mind. I was going to carry out my plan, and nothing would stop me.

As I shoved out the classroom door, I thought I saw Miss Switch looking at me with a strange, pale gleam in her eyes. I almost felt as if she was staring right through my brain and *reading* it! I shuddered as I hurried out of the school and on to the library.

"Let me see now . . . wisdom . . . wish . . . wit . . . *witch!* Ah, here we have it . . . witch. There you are, Rupert, a whole section on witches. I suppose you're doing this for school for Halloween? Funny, no one else has been looking for anything on that subject." Mrs. Brentwood, the librarian, looked puzzled.

"Oh no," I said. "It's not a school assignment. I'm just browsing around. You know."

"Oh yes," said Mrs. Brentwood, who didn't quite look as if she did know. "I guess this is as good a time as any to do some browsing on witches. You haven't run into one, I trust. Have you?" She gave me a confidential smile.

I smiled back and said nothing. I didn't want the conversation to go too far. Mrs. Brentwood was a pretty sharp person. I sometimes thought she used a little witchcraft herself when it came to finding the books I wanted. So even though I knew she was just having a little fun with me, I thought it was best to drop the conversation, and I sauntered away to the bookshelves with the list she had made for me.

For some reason, everything I had to look up was way in the back where it was dim and dusky. Some of the books on magic and sorcery looked as if they hadn't been touched in fifty-five years. I tried not to let this spooky situation bother me, and I went right to work.

Of course, I couldn't find a thing on the subject of spitballs or water fountains or anything along that line, but I found a lot of other information, and most of it made me very nervous. If Miss Switch was what I thought she was, there were all kinds of interesting things she could do, none of them good.

There was the business of taking something you

owned or was part of you, or was even something you'd written, and using it to cast some hideous spell on you. I didn't care for that at all. Had Miss Switch returned all my classroom papers? I couldn't remember.

I also found out that a witch could raise storms and ruin crops. Ruin crops? I thought of my aquarium with all the green stuff growing in the mason jars. I had two weeks' allowance invested in that.

But the most fearsome thing of all was a witch's ability to turn something into something else. Myself, for example. The thought of, say, Caruso, Hector, and Guinevere being turned into something like cows was bad enough. Three cows in my bedroom would present a large number of problems I didn't care to think about. But the thought of myself ending up as a toad or a lizard was the worst. What would my mother and father do about me? Would they want to introduce me as their son? Where would they keep me? Would I sit on the breakfast table watching my father feasting on fried eggs and cinnamon toast while I nibbled sadly on a fly or two? I couldn't bear the thought.

It was then I found something that raised my spirits tremendously. The information was in a book on folklore, and it described a kind of magic charm that could be used as a protection against witches. I had to admit to myself that I was grabbing at straws, but it was better than nothing, which was all I had at that moment. The magic charm was this:

When a witch sees her reflection in a mirror or in a pool of water, she should melt away completely.

Well, I knew I couldn't carry a pool of water around with me, but a small pocket mirror was easy to come by. What I would do would be to take one of these mirrors with me in my pocket when I finally had my meeting with Miss Switch. If she didn't listen to my gentlemanly reason and looked as if she might be going to cast a spell on me, I'd whip the mirror out of my jacket and hold it up to her face. That would do it! I smiled grimly.

I must have still been smiling grimly when I walked out of the library, because Mrs. Brentwood looked as if she thought I'd had an unpleasant experience in the book stacks.

At any rate, I hurried home and pulled out my notebook. I could feel my smile become even grimmer as I wrote down the following:

What: Mirror
Kind: Pocket
Whose: Mine
Performance: To be used against Miss Switch
    in case of need
How Tested: If Miss Switch melts away, it can
    then be considered a known way to prove
    scientifically

5

Midnight Expedition

At exactly twelve midnight, a faint buzz sounded in my room, and I sleepily reached under my pillow to turn off the alarm clock I'd hidden there. For a moment I lay wondering what I'd done a thing like that for, putting an alarm clock under my pillow. Then, when I remembered, I sat up suddenly, my skin tingling and my heart thudding.

I climbed stealthily out of bed and went over to the window to pull up the shade. The moon was full. It made deep, mysterious shadows in the garden. Shivering, I found the clothes I'd hidden under my bed and quickly pulled them on. As I climbed into my trousers, I felt the small, round mirror in the pocket. I wondered if I should take it with me and then finally decided that I might as well. Even though I'd made no plans to see Miss Switch, I'd agreed to myself earlier that I should keep the mirror with me at all times. That way I'd be protected against forgetting it, and I could always use it for reflecting the sun's rays into someone's eyes at school if I got bored. It was good insurance to have it along. I finished dressing quickly, picked up my flashlight from my desk, and tiptoed from the room and on into the hall, where I could hear the deep breathing of my father and mother which told me they were safely asleep. I turned on my flashlight, tiptoed on down the stairs and out of the house.

The school is only three blocks away from our house, but I took a shortcut I always used down a kind of dead-end street that leads up to the back end of the playground. When I reached the playground, I could see the school building looming like a gigantic, crouching animal across it. The moonlight striking each window made it seem like something with a thousand eyes. I wondered with a shudder if I could find the eye that was my room.

What I was doing there that night, of course, was to check out my schoolroom thoroughly before accusing Miss Switch of anything. If anyone were to ask me why I chose midnight to do it, I couldn't answer. Maybe it was because I considered it the proper time for an expert on witchcraft to carry out his research. Or maybe it was plain, ordinary stupidity. My truthful scientific nature leads me to confess that it was probably stupidity.

But who knew what I would discover. Maybe Miss Switch was just a very tricky teacher who had booby-trapped the room and the water fountain to mystify the class. I doubted it, but as a scientist I could leave no stones unturned.

I wished, though, that I'd picked some other time to come out besides midnight. If Miss Switch turned out to be nothing more than a smart magician, I was scaring myself to death for nothing. I wondered if I should have asked my father to come along with me. How would you go about asking your father to come out with you at midnight so that you could scale the walls of your school and enter a window to prowl around your classroom? It wouldn't be easy.

I wished I'd risked it, though, as I raced across the moonlit, shadowy playground all alone. I never felt more alone in all my life!

I didn't stop once until I reached the school building. Then I stood there, panting and shivering at the same time, while I counted from the end of the building to find my room, Room Twenty. I was pretty sure that one window would be unlocked because I'd observed earlier that the latch on it wasn't working too well and no one had got around to fixing it. At least, I hoped no one had.

Room Twenty was on the first floor, and it wasn't too difficult to put my fingers on the windowsill and hoist myself up. But I was so busy climbing and trying to push open the window that I failed to notice something. What had seemed like the reflection of the moon on the window, just as the moon was reflecting on all the other windows, was more the reflection of a small light from *inside*. It was a small light that was casting a dim, eerie glow all through the classroom.

It was only when I'd climbed through the window and had both feet securely on the floor inside that I looked up and saw the light burning on the teacher's desk. I stood frozen to the spot where my feet had touched ground. My blood felt as if it had turned to ice water. I hoped I'd faint and wake up back in my room. But I didn't. I just stood and stared.

Sitting on the desk was the largest black cat I'd ever seen. It had great wide, slanted eyes that seemed to be made of green glass. It had a long tail that it was flicking from side to side. For a moment the cat stared back at me, then it returned to washing its whiskers as if I weren't even there.

Directly in front of the cat was a small flame. The flame came from a Bunsen burner that the class sometimes used for experiments.

And standing over the Bunsen burner was a figure!

It had on a black cape, and on its head a tall, pointed black hat whose shadow, cast by the burner, flickered over the blackboard as if it were licking off the chalk dust. The figure dressed in black had eyes almost like those of the cat, green and slanted and like glass. And they sent off sparks that danced over the desk like burning gold.

"Good evening, Rupert!" said Miss Switch.

6

The Trouble with Miss Switch

My speech was forgotten. My low bow from the waist was forgotten. I was scared stiff!

"Good evening!" Miss Switch said again. "Well, don't just stand there. After all, I've been expecting you. Don't keep me waiting any longer."

"E . . . e . . . expecting me?" I croaked.

I tried to walk forward, but I had to grab a desk because my legs were behaving very strangely.

"Certainly," said Miss Switch. "You don't actually think I haven't known what you've been up to, do you?"

I had the feeling that Miss Switch was trying to look pleasant. She was smiling, anyway, so I moved a few feet closer to the desk.

"Well, why didn't you do something about it?" I asked.

Miss Switch's smile grew broader and thinner. "*Do* something? Why, I have no intention of doing anything at all."

I fell down into the nearest desk, which just happened to be mine. "You don't?"

"Certainly not! Why should I, after all the trouble I've had getting you here?"

I felt my jaw fall open. "You mean to say you *wanted* me to find out about you?"

"You might put it that way," said Miss Switch, rubbing her hands over the Bunsen burner.

"Well, why didn't you just *tell* me about it?" I sounded annoyed, but I guess all I could think of was my wasted scientific effort. Heck, I thought—all those notes I'd made!

Miss Switch's eyes flashed dangerously. "How far would I have got if I'd just come up and announced to you that I was what I was without letting you find it out for yourself?"

"I guess you're right," I replied, after thinking

the question over. "Not very far at all. I probably would have thought you were suffering from . . . er . . . bats in your belfry, Miss Switch. Still, it's going to take me a while to get used to this whole idea."

For a few minutes Miss Switch seemed to go off into a trance, staring at the burner. Then she gave a low, hoarse chuckle. "Hadn't expected it to turn out this way, eh? On your way to tell the authorities, eh?" She gave another chuckle which sounded more like a cackle, interesting but not very safe. I fingered the mirror in my pants pocket.

"Oh, I wasn't really going to do anything like that," I said quickly. "What I mean is, I thought I ought to hear your side of the situation first. It's not that what you've done has hurt anyone or anything like that. It's what you might do that worries me. According to what I read in the library and my notes . . ."

"Confound it, stop being so scientific," grumbled Miss Switch. "I have science coming out my ears. If it weren't for science . . ." She stopped her sentence in the middle and gave me a glassy green stare.

I waited for her to finish that curious remark, but she didn't. Instead, she walked over and squeezed into a desk next to mine. It happened to be Amelia Daley's desk. Then she leaned way over and gave me a very confidential look. "Actually, you don't have to worry about a thing," she said. "I have no intention of doing anything wicked at all. And after all, when you stop to consider it, the only witchcraft I've practiced in class is just to make things a little easier on myself. It hasn't harmed anyone, as you've seen, and you have to admit that it keeps the class in line."

"Yes, it does," I said thoughtfully.

"Well, then, aside from all that poppycock you've been studying, what makes you think I'm going to be up to anything worse?"

"I don't really know," I said. "Maybe it's just that Halloween is coming."

"Halloween? Oh fiddlesticks!" snorted Miss Switch. Her green eyes shot out sparks that burned holes in Amelia's desk. "All we witches do on Halloween is have a bit of innocent fun, a bit of pleasure. You wouldn't begrudge us that, would you? You know, a little dancing hither and yon, a bit of gaiety, a mad flight through the moonlight. What harm is there in that?"

"None, when you put it that way," I admitted.

44

"But I'll still have to think about it."

"Think away!" said Miss Switch.

"Besides," I continued, "you haven't told me yet why you wanted me to find out about you. That still seems pretty strange to me."

"Nothing strange about it at all. The fact is that even though I don't have much use for science at the moment, a likely lad with a scientific brain like yours could be just the one to offer me the assistance I need." Miss Switch edged her face close to mine and dropped her voice. "And if you must know, I'm not here just to pass the time of day."

"I didn't think so," I said.

"No, I'm here to perform a certain kind of witchcraft."

"Aha!" I exclaimed, unable to restrain myself.

"Aha yourself! There you go, jumping to the wrong conclusions, assuming that it's going to be *wicked* witchcraft. Where are your powers of deduction, Rupert? I should think you would have been able to figure out arithmetically, if not scientifically, from what I've already done that I'm not planning to ruin someone's life. But, come to think of it, your arithmetic has been very poor lately. I think this might be a good time to go over some of your papers." Miss Switch leaned way over the arm of Amelia's desk and began to rummage around in the papers under my own.

"Heck, Miss Switch," I said, "do we have to do that now?" I have to admit that it was reassuring to be reminded that this was still good old Miss Switch, my teacher, I was talking to, but after all, I hadn't crawled out of bed at midnight to discuss *arithmetic* papers!

Miss Switch looked startled, as if she'd forgotten herself. "Oh, all right," she said grumpily. "Now, where were we?"

"We were talking about why you were here, Miss Switch. Why *are* you here? I mean, why do you have to perform . . . uh . . . a certain kind of witchcraft?"

Miss Switch edged her face uncomfortably close to mine. Her voice became even lower and more confidential. "Well, you might as well know it. I've been put on probation!"

"What's that supposed to mean?" I asked.

To my surprise, Miss Switch gave a deep sigh. For a moment she looked almost human. "I just don't know what's happening in the world. All the old familiar ways going down the drain. The fact is,

Rupert, that progress, if you can call it that, has reached the witch's kingdom. Oh, I don't mind being a bit modern and giving up some of those old horrors we used to be noted for. But now, thanks to your beloved science, we're being dictated to by a . . . by a blasted computowitch!"

"A computo-*what*?" I gasped.

"A computo-*witch*, Rupert. A computer for witches." Miss Switch shook her head sadly. "Here I was happily buzzing about on my broomstick, scaring a few people, howling at the moon, rattling a bone or two. Now, thanks to some idiot on the Witches' Council who thinks that we're not modern enough, that we're not keeping up with the times, my life is being disrupted by a confounded machine!"

I was hardly hearing Miss Switch. My mind had gone into a trance. A computowitch! Science meets witchcraft! My brain was doing cartwheels.

"How does a thing like that work?" I asked, trying not to sound too eager.

"It works just like any other silly computer, I guess," Miss Switch grumbled. "It's just restricted to information on witches, that's all. And if you must know, I don't care to have my personal history analyzed by a pile of nuts and bolts. I had to have it done, though. We all did."

"That's too bad," I said sympathetically.

"It was for me," Miss Switch growled. "As it turned out, there was just one person who came out with a minus in front of her name, one person who didn't measure up." Miss Switch rose from Amelia's desk and strode to the window.

"You?" I suggested meekly.

"Who else?" she said.

"Oh," I said.

"Oh, indeed," she said. "Unoriginal! My card came out of that miserable machine saying *old hat!* Unoriginal! Put on probation!"

"You've been pretty original in the classroom, Miss Switch," I said.

She ignored my remark. "Well, I'd better come up with something and carry it out successfully . . . or else!"

"Or else what?"

"Punishment, naturally. How would you feel, Rupert, if you were a witch banished to Witch's Mountain, there to do nothing with your broomstick for one hundred and fifty years but—*sweep!*"

"I'd feel terrible," I said.

"Exactly!" snorted Miss Switch.

"But I still don't see where I come into all this," I said.

Miss Switch walked over to my desk, leaned down on it, and looked straight into my eyes. Uh oh! I said to myself. What's this all about? I felt her stare, glassy and green, boring into my brain. I began to feel a little dizzy.

"What you can do, dear boy," Miss Switch said smoothly, "is to help me think up an original act of witchcraft. After all, a boy with your fertile scientific brain should be able to help me out, eh?"

Suddenly I didn't like the way Miss Switch was sounding. It made me very nervous. What would I be getting into if I said yes? A pact with a witch! Wasn't that a sinister, dangerous arrangement? Forget the computowitch! Forget the whole thing! Tell Miss Switch you'll never say a word to the authorities. Tell her to get herself another boy. She has a whole class to choose from. Recommend Peatmouse. Recommend anybody! Just say no thanks and good-night and leave while you're still alive.

Miss Switch must have been reading my mind because suddenly she threw her head back with a loud cackle followed by a hissing noise. My head began to whirl, round and round, spinning and spinning, dizzier and dizzier, while my stomach felt as if it had collapsed to nothing. It was all my own fault, allowing myself to get into this spot where I could be bewitched, probably being turned into something at that very moment.

Good-bye! Good-bye Mother and Dad! Good-bye Banana, Peatmouse, and Creampuff! Farewell Pepperdine P. S.! Good-bye my archenemy Amelia Daley even! Good-bye world! The next time I look at you if may be through the eyes of a frog or a hairy caterpillar!

Then I remembered it—the mirror! Somehow the message spun through my fogged-up brain. Get the mirror and get it fast. I reached into my pocket and dragged it out.

"Look into this, Miss Switch!" I commanded.

"Oh put that thing away. It's just another silly superstition. I should think you'd be ashamed with your scientific mind believing in that kind of nonsense. Why, I thought that sort of thing went out with long skirts—or is it short skirts?"

I wasn't going to be fooled. "Look into it!" I roared.

Miss Switch did, and immediately started to arrange her hat as if she were trying it on in a hat shop. She didn't melt away or anything.

"Oh heck!" I said, pocketing the mirror.

"Well, come, come, Rupert, now that we've gone through that bit of silliness, are you or are you not going to help me?"

I felt like a real dumbbell. "Oh sure, I guess so," I said lamely.

"Splendid!" Miss Switch said with a brisk swish of her skirts. "I knew you wouldn't fail me. When you've thought of something, simply leave a note on my desk and I'll make arrangements to meet with you. You can run along now. It's way past your bedtime. Say goodnight, Bathsheba."

"Goodnight," the black cat said, nodding in my direction.

Good gravy! I thought. A talking cat! What next?

I rose, but I didn't move because there was still something I had to know.

"I said goodnight," Miss Switch reminded me sharply.

I decided to come right out with it. "Miss Switch, what I don't understand is why you're here. I mean, why do you have to be a teacher of my fifth grade class at Pepperdine while you're performing your original witchcraft?"

"Can't you guess?" said Miss Switch.

"The computowitch?"

"What else? You don't think anybody in their right mind would have chosen the job, do you?"

"I guess not," I said. "Well, goodnight again."

"Goodnight, Rupert!"

Poor Miss Switch, I said to myself on the way home. Being ordered by a *computer* to teach my fifth grade class. Under the circumstances I wouldn't have blamed her if she'd been a miserable teacher. But she wasn't! How could I have even considered failing her and seeing her sentenced to sweeping a mountain for one hundred and fifty years? What kind of a kid would I be to let a thing like that happen to a nice person like Miss Switch?

At any rate, when I crawled back into my bed a short time later, I was too worn out to think about anything, scientifically or otherwise. And for the first time in many nights, I made no notes in my notebook.

7

Original Witchcraft

My head had no more hit the pillow when some strange sounds began to drift into my ears. There were two kinds of groaning sounds, one in a low register. A third sound, very high and very thin, as if it were coming from a tiny flute, rose above both the groaning sounds. Furthermore, in the third sound I could detect words. This sound, or voice, was actually singing something that sounded like "O Solo Mio."

My first thought was that I'd left on my pocket radio, but then I realized that my radio was by my bed and these sounds were coming from where my experiments were, across the room. I threw myself out of bed, grabbed my flashlight, and shone it on Hector, Guinevere, and Caruso. The singing, which was coming from Caruso, came to a sudden stop.

"Well, don't just stand there with your jaw hanging open," I heard Caruso say in a thin, musical voice. "Can't you speak?"

"I don't know. I mean, *sure* I can speak!" I said.

"Well then, why aren't you saying anything?" he asked.

"I don't know what to say," I replied. "What I mean is, look, I've never talked to a turtle before." I fell into the chair by my desk because my knees were getting too weak to carry me.

"Live and learn," Caruso said, and he burst into song again.

"Aren't you going to ask why we're groaning?" asked a voice from my guinea pig cage.

"I hadn't thought about it," I said. "But now that you mention it, why *are* you groaning?"

"I'm starved," said Hector.

"I'm stuffed," said Guinevere.

"I'm sorry," I said. "I suppose being a nutrition experiment isn't the easiest thing in the world."

"*You're* telling *us!*" Hector and Guinevere groaned in unison.

"What I'd like to know is how long this thing has to continue," Hector said. "As I see it, if you don't do something about us very soon, one of three things can happen. I'll die of malnutrition . . ."

"Or I'll explode," said Guinevere.

"Or both," Hector concluded.

"Why haven't you mentioned all this before?" I asked, realizing at once that it wasn't a very bright question.

"That wasn't a very bright question," said Caruso, ending his aria. "Now how could they?"

"You're right," I said, "they couldn't. The point is, how can we all talk to each other now? There's no scientific explanation for this sort of thing as far as I know."

"That just leaves one other," Caruso said. "The nearest I can come to figuring it is that you've run into some kind of sorcerer or other. This kind of thing happens when you have dealings with certain kinds of people. You know," he said, lowering his voice, *"witchcraft!"*

"That's it, of course. Witchcraft!" I exclaimed. "As a matter of fact, I have entered into a kind of . . . well, an arrangement with a witch."

"Aha!" Caruso said. He put his front feet on one claw. "I suspected something of the sort. Well, I only hope for your sake it's a pleasant one. Witches don't have a very good reputation, as I recall it."

"Oh, I think this one is going to be all right," I hurried to say. "Miss Switch is sort of a modern witch. She's also my fifth grade teacher at Pepperdine, which is how I ran into her."

"Hmmmm, very interesting," Caruso said.

"It all came about because she's in trouble and needs help. She's been put on probation by something called a computowitch. That's a computer for witches. It's pretty complicated and I don't think you'd understand if I tried to explain it."

"You don't need to," Caruso said in an injured voice. "I know what a computer is. Witches aren't the only ones. There's such a thing as a modern turtle, in case you're interested."

"I am interested," I said. "And I'm sorry about what I said."

"Oh, that's all right. What I don't understand, though, is where you fit into all this."

"Well, the computowitch has ordered her to come up with some kind of original witchcraft or do nothing but sweep Witch's Mountain for one hundred and fifty years."

"Wheee-ooo!" Caruso whistled. "That would be a pretty long time even for a turtle."

"You bet it would!" I said. "Anyway, with my fertile scientific brain and all that, Miss Switch thinks I might be the one to help her come up with a bright witchcraft idea or two."

"How about your saxophone?" Hector asked.

"What about my saxophone?"

"He means that teaching you to blow your saxophone might be some pretty original witchcraft," Caruso interrupted. "It would certainly be a boon to the animal world if nothing else. The noises you make are absolutely ear-splitting."

"Oh, so you *do* have ears," I said. "I've often wondered about that."

"Yes, and when it comes to your saxophone practice, I often wish I didn't," Caruso said. "At any rate, I think you should seriously consider having your witch friend work some magic in that department. Instant sax success through sorcery. A rather good idea, if I do say so."

I thought this over carefully. "You know something? That gives me an even better idea—not about the saxophone, but something else that Miss Switch could do with music."

"Carry on," said Caruso.

"Well, our school band is going to play at the next football game. Boy, are they rotten! The thing is that it's our big game of the year with Dinwiddie School and a lot of people will be there, mothers and dads and all that. We're going to try to raise some money to buy band uniforms. Now, if Miss Switch could just do something to make the band play like it knew what it was doing for once, we might pass the hat and make a lot extra."

"I hope it works," Hector said. "If it doesn't, you might have people demanding their money *back*. Even parents have their limitations, you know."

Caruso yawned. "Personally, that doesn't sound like my idea of witchcraft—a school band concert. I wonder if the computowitch would accept that. Is that the best your fertile scientific brain can come up with?"

"Have you got any better ideas?" I asked.

"Well, when you put it that way, no." Caruso

began to hum the opening bars of "Stars and Stripes Forever." "By the way, what are Pepperdine's chances this Saturday?"

"Are you kidding?" I said. "Pepperdine has never beat Dinwiddie in its whole history. Our football team is worse than the band. It would really take something unbelievable for Pepperdine to win this week."

"Like witchcraft?" Caruso said.

"It would have to be pretty original."

"Then there you are!" Caruso exclaimed.

"There I am what?"

"There you are, there's something for your fertile scientific brain to go to work on. And you have to admit that as far as making money is concerned, people would be willing to shell out a lot more to see Pepperdine beat Dinwiddie than to hear the Peppy P. S. band render a couple of tired marching tunes, good or otherwise."

"You're probably right," I admitted. "The problem is what kind of witchcraft do you use in a football game that wouldn't look like cheating?"

"I'm afraid that's your problem," Caruso advised me. "I'm only a turtle, not a member of the National Football Rules Association. Or a magician either. The only tricks I could suggest are the things I've seen you perform from your amateur magic set—a couple of tired card tricks, the old shell game you never have been able to do because you keep losing the pea, and the disappearing ball act. You're not too bad at that one."

"Hey!" I shouted. "Wait a minute! Wait . . . a . . . minute! How about a disappearing ball *and* quarterback? No passing necessary. The quarterback gets the ball. They both disappear. Touchdown! Heck, half the people never can follow the ball at a Pepperdine game anyway. The other half would think they needed glasses. It ought to look pretty good."

"Bravo!" shouted Guinevere, sounding a little strangled because her mouth was stuffed with guinea pig feed. "There you are, I knew you'd do it!"

"Sounds fine to me," said Hector.

"It might pass," said Caruso.

"There's still one thing that worries me, though. It may not *look* like cheating, but that doesn't mean it isn't. I'm afraid I'll have to think about this further."

"You do that," said Caruso. "I personally have thought all I'm going to this evening. If you don't mind, I'm going to sing myself a little lullaby and turn in."

"I think I will too," Hector added. "But before I do, might I make a suggestion?"

"Certainly."

"Would you be kind enough to consider an immediate dietary change for your nutrition experiment? As things are going, I might not last the night."

"And what's more," Guinevere said, "another gorge for breakfast and I might not last the meal. Self-control has never been a strong point with me. If you put it in front of me, I eat it. You may have noticed."

"I have noted it," I told her as I reached into the cages and changed the feed bowls.

Guinevere greeted the change with a huge sigh of delight. "It's a pleasure to be served a meal I can't stand the sight of."

"I won't carry things so far again," I promised.

"Well, goodnight, Rupert," said Caruso.

"Goodnight."

"Goodnight, Rupert," said Hector and Guinevere.

"Goodnight," I said, and fell into bed. When I

dropped off to sleep at last, I could still hear the soft strains of "Brahms' Lullaby" sung in a thin, piping voice come drifting across the dark room to my bed.

8

The Bewitching

I nearly fell asleep at my desk the next day. That was when I found out that Miss Switch the teacher wasn't going to let me get away with anything just because I had an agreement with Miss Switch the witch. She gave me a nasty look every time I yawned, which was often. And once, when I sleepily snapped a rubber band on Peatmouse's ear, I felt a sharp sting on my own. Whatever I was getting out of all my trouble, it certainly wasn't any advantages in the classroom!

At any rate, I'd finally decided that I should

63

present the football game idea to Miss Switch, so the first chance I got, I tore off the corner of an English paper and scribbled a note on it: "I have a possible idea. Please advise." Then I sauntered over to Miss Switch's desk during free period and dropped it in front of her.

I never did see her pick up the note or read it, but about the time I'd decided I was dreaming the whole thing, I heard her call out my name. "Rupert! Your handwriting shows no improvement whatsoever. Please see me immediately after school." Several members of the class looked at me with sympathy, and I tried to look miserable.

The minute the last person in the class had departed after the closing bell, I presented myself to Miss Switch at her desk. Her green eyes flashed approvingly. "Now, Rupert, about your handwriting . . ." she began. Then she dropped her voice. "Come along! Out with it! What's this idea of yours?" Sparks flew out from her eyes and sizzled on her desk.

I outlined my plan to her.

When I'd finished, she rose from her desk and marched back and forth in front of it, her hands behind her back. "Hmmm," I heard her muttering, "a disappearing ball and quarterback! That sounds original enough. And Pepperdine beating Dinwiddie? That is original *indeed*. Yes, Rupert! Splendid! I think it can be done. This should set that blasted computowitch back on its heels." She sat down at her desk again and began to drum on it with her long fingers, a thin, pleased smile on her face.

"Miss Switch?" I began hesitantly.

"Well, what's wrong?"

"Miss Switch," I repeated firmly. "The reason I put down 'possible idea' in my note is that I don't want to do anything that's cheating. I'm not sure if having the quarterback and ball disappear would be breaking the rules."

Miss Switch drummed harder on the desk. "Well, Rupert, would you please be kind enough to explain to me all the football rules dealing with witchcraft?"

"I can't," I said. "There aren't any."

"Well then," she snapped, "if the football people haven't the intelligence to include witchcraft in their rules, that's *their* problem. And as far as I can see, you can't very well break a rule that's never been made. At any rate, I intend to go ahead with this whether you like it or not. Now, Rupert, who is this quarterback we're going to make disappear?"

I wasn't quite convinced about the whole thing, but since I'd presented the idea and Miss Switch was going to go ahead with it anyway, there wasn't much for me to do but follow along. "It's Harvey Fanna," I said. "His number is fifteen."

Miss Switch rubbed her chin thoughtfully. "Fifteen, eh? Yes, we'll simply bewitch the number fifteen. He'll disappear each time he gets the ball, then reappear as soon as he's made the touchdown. I should have no trouble with that at all. Now, you understand, Rupert, that I shall want you at the bewitching tonight."

"Me?" I managed to gasp out.

"Certainly, you," said Miss Switch. "And of course I shall also want a few ingredients. Nothing complicated—just a bit of crumbled toadstool, a half of a bat wing, and one newt's eye. Would you try the druggist right away and let me know what you can do? I should hate to have to go after these things myself."

"Do you really need all those things, Miss Switch?" I asked. "I mean, aren't they all a little old-fashioned, like the mirror?"

Miss Switch gave me a fierce look filled with annoyance. "Certainly they're old-fashioned! I just use them by way of precaution. A little insurance never hurt anyone. And after all, the old remedies are the best remedies."

"So I've heard," I said.

"Well, then, get on with it. And stop off on the way home and let me know how you've done. I'll be here correcting papers, of course. I expect to find the results of the day's arithmetic test a total disaster."

I didn't care to stop and discuss the results of the day's arithmetic test, especially my own, so I hurried to the door. When I reached it, however, I hesitated.

"Well, what's wrong now, Rupert?"

"Miss Switch, do you suppose that while you're bewitching the quarterback, you could also bewitch the Pepperdine school band just enough so they'd play a couple of decent pieces at the game? It would help them get their new uniforms, and I could leave my earmuffs at home."

Miss Switch didn't hesitate a moment. "Certainly, Rupert, I shall be glad to be of service to you and Pepperdine. Now hurry along, please."

Somehow I felt a lot better about the whole arrangement after this, and I hurried on to the drugstore to make my request of Mr. Henry, the druggist.

After Mr. Henry had heard it, he rubbed his chin thoughtfully. "I haven't had any call for those items in quite some time," he said. "But let me look in my stock and see what I can do." He disappeared into the back room, leaving me to examine the labels of everything in the store and marvel at the opportunities a scientist could have if he were turned loose in there. Also while I was waiting I helped myself to a free squirt of cologne and two toothpicks.

Mr. Henry finally returned, shaking his head. "Nope, sorry, Rupert, not a toadstool in the house. Can't remember when we had our last bat wing, either. As for newt's eyes, well, they've been scarcer than hen's teeth. Could I interest you in a peppermint stick?" I reached into the jar that he handed me and pulled out a stick of red and white striped candy.

"Thanks anyway, Mr. Henry," I said.

Of course I knew that Mr. Henry was just putting me on, but I also knew I had to do as Miss

Switch had requested. Anyway, I felt that the cologne, toothpicks, and peppermint stick were worth the trip.

"Oh blast and botheration!" Miss Switch said when I returned to the classroom with only a peppermint stick in my hand. She chewed furiously on her pencil. "I'll just have to get the things myself—except the toadstools. I'll expect you to pick those up on your way here tonight. You certainly can't have any trouble with that!"

I could think of a lot of trouble I could have gathering toadstools at midnight, but with the kind of look Miss Switch gave me, I didn't care to mention it. So at midnight that night, with a small paper sack in one hand and flashlight in the other, I was out looking for toadstools in back of the school playground. Fortunately, I was able to find several good, moldy-looking specimens.

Miss Switch was waiting for me in the classroom when I climbed in through the window.

"I never thought he'd make it," said Bathsheba, who was already at work on her whiskers.

"Sssssss!" Miss Switch hissed at her. "Mind your own business, cat! Now, Rupert, let's see what you've brought."

I took a deep breath as Miss Switch, once again in her long black cloak and tall, pointed hat, peered into the paper sack.

"Splendid!" she said. "I don't see any reason now why we can't begin at once." She began to wave her hands slowly over the Bunsen burner. "Now, Rupert, when I call for the ingredients, hand them to me. And stand back!"

"Miss Switch, you won't forget the band, will you?" I cried out.

"My pleasure," she said, and with that began swooping back and forth in front of her desk, calling out strange, unearthly words, dancing with her arms over her head, and making wild cries over the burner.

"Toadstools!" she shouted at me, and I handed them to her.

"Wing of bat!" she howled, and I obliged her with that, too.

"Eye of newt!" she screamed, and there I was with it.

Then she hurled everything into the Bunsen burner, and as each burned up to a fiery crisp she cried out,

"Fifteen, fifteen, disappear,
Band will play and soothe the ear,
Ball will reach and then be nought,
Until the irking fight is fought!"

I didn't think Miss Switch's poetry was outstanding, but it was the most exciting show of its kind I'd ever seen.

When it was ended, Miss Switch threw herself into the chair at her desk, panting and fanning herself with her hand.

"Is that all, Miss Switch?" I asked.

"Certainly that's all!" she snapped.

"Well then, should I go home now?"

"Run along!"

I started toward the window.

"Rupert!"

"Yes, Miss Switch?"

"Please don't slouch when you walk. You children *must* learn to stand up straight!"

"Yes, Miss Switch," I said.

9

Pepperdine vs. Dinwiddie

I rose early Saturday and immediately after breakfast went to Banana's house to make sure that he was all right. He was asleep, but Mrs. Fanna assured me that he was well and planning to play in the game that day.

I returned there twice again, and finally Mrs. Fanna took me up to Banana's room to see for myself that he was just sleeping and not dead. Mrs. Fanna looked at me rather strangely, but I wasn't surprised because Banana has informed me that his mother has always called me "Harvey's strange little scientific friend."

Later in the morning I went to the school to help set up folding chairs and then, with the help of Creampuff and Peatmouse, spent the rest of the time bothering the band, getting in the way of the practicing football players, and annoying the school custodian by asking what I could do to help.

"Here, come taste the punch, Rupert," one of the mothers called. I did, and that together with setting up chairs was probably the only useful thing I did all morning. I don't think I need to mention, however, that I was very impatient, and all this helped to pass the time until the start of the game.

In any event, at one thirty my father and mother and I were standing in line for tickets. The game started at two, but I wanted to be sure to get a front row seat. We had just sat down when I saw Miss Switch arrive. I beckoned to her and she came and sat down beside me. My mother and father looked at one another as if to say, "Rupert's teacher's sitting with Rupert! Well!"

"Do you think it's going to work?" I whispered to Miss Switch.

"Of course it's going to work!" she hissed in my ear. Then she leaned around me and looked at my mother. "Lovely day for a game," she said.

People piled in, punch was poured and passed over everyone, pandemonium reigned, and the football teams ran out on the field. "Rah! Rah!" shouted a few Pepperdine people. Dinwiddie's side of the field was naturally screaming its head off, but it was difficult to be excited over the Pepperdine team.

I wasn't looking for anything but one thing—number fifteen on a red and white jersey, Pepperdine's colors, and it was there! "Rah! Rah!" I yelled happily.

"Rah! Rah!" shouted the cheering section which was sitting on the grass in front of the folding chairs. Amelia Daley kept turning around and giving Miss Switch and me long looks. She was sitting with the cheering section. I tried to ignore her, but I had to admit to myself that she looked rather nice that day—for a snoop, that is.

The cheering section began to liven up.

"Rah! Rah! For Peppy P. S.
Of all the schools we like you best,

If you win or if you lose,
You're the one we'll always choose!"

"Rah!" I said.

"Rah!" said Miss Switch.

And the game began.

It went exactly as we had planned it—for the first two minutes. Pepperdine got the ball. They huddled. The ball was passed to number fifteen who, together with the ball, promptly disappeared and then reappeared on the other side of Dinwiddie's goal line. The Dinwiddie side of the field was stunned and silent while Pepperdine went wild. Miss Switch and I shook hands triumphantly. Pepperdine didn't make the extra point when they kicked. They never had made it. Neither had Dinwiddie, but then I wasn't worried about that anyway. The score stood at six to nothing.

Then came the kick-off and it was Dinwiddie's ball. Almost all I'd done the whole time was keep my eyes on red and white number fifteen, but when Dinwiddie huddled, I managed to let my glance drift off for a moment to their quarterback to see what our defense was up against. Then I took off my glasses, polished them on my trousers, and put them on again. Number fifteen! The jersey was purple and yellow, but the number was fifteen! Miss Switch saw it, too, at exactly the same moment.

"Blast!" I heard her mutter. "It must have been the bat wing. I thought it had a musty odor about it!"

"But, Miss Switch," I whispered, "I thought you said those things were old-fashioned and didn't really have anything to do with all this."

"Of course I did!" she snapped. "But I have to blame something instead of my own stupidity. Bewitching the number instead of the boy! Blast and botheration!"

"What do we do now, Miss Switch?" I asked.

"Pray!"

Well, I prayed, but it didn't do any good. I watched in horror as the Dinwiddie quarterback received the ball, disappeared, and didn't appear again until he'd crossed the goal line. Dinwiddie didn't make the extra point either, as usual, but that didn't keep the Dinwiddie side from roaring while Pepperdine fell silent. The score was now six to six.

Back and forth went the ball from one team to the other. Touchdown after touchdown was made. The score went up like stairs, Pepperdine and then Dinwiddie and then Pepperdine. I began to review in my mind what the possible outcome of the game could be as things were going. If Pepperdine was the last team to have the ball before the final gun, they'd win. If Dinwiddie was the last to have the ball, it would be a tie. So, I reasoned, the worst that could happen to us would be a tied game. Once I arrived at this conclusion, I settled down to enjoy myself.

Touchdown after touchdown. Touchdown after touchdown. Back and forth, back and forth—the teams kept on making them one after the other. When the scores had passed sixty, it began to get boring. People almost stopped cheering when a touchdown was made. When it was our side, only a few people in the cheering section managed to say half-heartedly,

> "Rah! Rah! Rah! For Peppy P.
> There's no other place else we'd rather be,
> Gosh oh golly, gosh oh gee,
> We will always think of thee!"

It was so boring that some Dinwiddie rooters even came over to sample the Pepperdine punch, and vice versa.

With one minute left to play, the score stood at ninety-six to ninety, and it was Dinwiddie's ball. I never stopped hoping that Pepperdine would be the last one to have it, but even if we only tied Dinwiddie, it was better than anything we'd ever done before. Dinwiddie made the touchdown, as I expected. The score was ninety-six to ninety-six. I stood up to leave, and then it happened. Dinwiddie kicked for the extra point and made it! It couldn't have happened, but it did. I sat back down with a thud and stared with disbelief as the Dinwiddie rooters gleefully marched their team off the field. The score—ninety-six to ninety-seven—them, and the game ended!

I turned in horror to say something to Miss Switch, and she was gone!

10

Amelia Daley

I was so worried I barely heard my father's voice saying to me on the way home, "By the way, what happened to the band today, Rupert?"

"Yes," my mother added, "they were splendid. I'm sure their playing helped the school earn enough money for band uniforms when the hat was passed. You mustn't be too despondent about losing the game, dear. The band really made up for it, and after all, there will be other games with Dinwiddie, you know."

"Not like this one," I said.

"True," said my father. "It was rather unusual. I've never been to a game with so many touchdowns in my life. One things that puzzles me, though, is the way I kept losing sight of the quarterbacks and the balls once they'd received them. I suppose I need to get my glasses checked."

"Why, now that you mention it, I think I do too," said my mother. "Were you able to keep track of everything, dear?"

"Not exactly," I replied.

"What do you mean by not exactly?" said my father.

"I meant no," I said.

"I thought that's what you meant," said my father.

"Well then," my mother said, "I suppose we'll *all* need to go and get our glasses checked."

"I suppose so," I said.

Well, after all, it was a lot easier to get my glasses checked than to try and explain about toadstools, bat wings, and eye of newt. I would have ended up getting my head checked instead of my glasses. I didn't see any point in going into it.

The moment we arrived home I raced up to my room.

"Miss Switch has gone! Miss Switch has gone!" I cried.

"Take it easy!" said Caruso. "She can't have gone very far. Or if she has, she's certainly coming back again."

"How do you know that?" I asked.

"Well, we're still talking to each other, aren't we? That must mean that she still has the arrangement with you. And as long as she does, I would think you'd have to see her again."

"That's right!" I exclaimed, wondering why I hadn't thought of it myself. It certainly proved to me that a turtle could be more intelligent than a human at times. "But I wonder why she left without saying anything to me?"

"Maybe she did," Caruso mused. "Did you check your pockets for messages or anything of that sort?"

I picked up my jacket which I'd thrown on the bed and began to feel about in the pockets. "Here it is! Here's something!" I said, excitedly drawing out a small piece of folded black paper from the pocket that had been nearest Miss Switch when we were at the game.

"Don't just stand there holding it! Open it and see what it says," Hector said.

I unfolded the piece of paper and slowly read aloud the words written on it in a luminous yellow ink: "Returning to W. M. to see Cptw. Meet with me Monday during recess about your handwriting. M. S."

"There you are!" said Guinevere. "I knew she wouldn't just go off without saying anything."

"W. M.? Cptw.?" I mumbled.

"Don't be dense, Rupert," said Caruso. "She's gone off to Witch's Mountain to get a report from the computowitch, of course. I hope it's a good one. By the way, how *did* things go today at the game?"

"Oh yes, please do tell us!" Guinevere cried. "I'm simply dying to know."

I shook my head sadly. "Not at all well, I'm afraid. We lost!"

"LOST!" the three animals exclaimed.

"How did *that* happen?" Caruso nearly fell out of his bowl.

"Who knows? I'm just a fifth grade scientist, not a witch. Maybe it was the musty bat wing after all. Anyway, this is what happened . . ." I told them the whole story of the game that day.

"The thing is," I concluded, "when you get

right down to it, it's only losing a football game to me, and at that it's the best we've ever done against Dinwiddie. But Miss Switch was ordered to perform an act of original witchcraft *successfully*. That game could put Miss Switch behind the broom on Witch's Mountain for one hundred and fifty years!"

Guinevere gasped, "How awful!"

"Yes, it is," said Caruso. "At any rate, you won't be left wondering long what the outcome of this is going to be. And it's a good thing you have us around to talk it over with."

"You're right about that," I said. "What would I have done if I'd come home and found that you couldn't talk to me anymore? Who could I have talked to about it? Who would have believed me?"

"*I* would!" said a voice from the doorway.

It was the voice of Amelia, the snoop.

"What are you doing here?" I said, trying not to sound as if I was inviting her into my room. She came in anyway.

"Your mother said I could see you," she said.

I couldn't think of a thing to say to that, and for a minute all I did was stand and stare with my mouth hanging open, watching Amelia as she sat down on the floor and pushed her silly brown curls away from her face. I felt as if I was hypnotized, as if my whole self had just stopped working. When I was finally able to speak, it was a surprise to hear my own voice. It didn't even sound like my own voice.

"What do you mean, '*I* would'?" I asked. "What are you talking about?"

"You know very well what I'm talking about, Rupert Brown! While you've been watching Miss Switch, I've been watching *you* and Miss Switch!"

So! I'd been right about Amelia. I should have had my eye on her all along—both eyes. A scientist really should have eyes on the back of his head, I advised myself. That snoop! That snoopy Amelia Daley! I couldn't get over it.

"At any rate," Amelia went on, "I wasn't really sure about anything until just now when I heard you talking to someone." She looked carefully around the room. "Who were you talking to?"

"I don't have to tell you," I said.

"I don't care if you do or you don't. Besides, I already know everything I want to know!" She bobbed her head at me, and the silly curls flew all over her forehead. "I've suspected that Miss Switch was a witch all along. I knew that you suspected it

84

too, but you'd never talk about it to me. And I saw you two whispering at the football game, and then everything happened with the disappearing quarterbacks. I knew that they'd *really* disappeared and that it was witchcraft and not just because everyone needed their glasses checked!"

"Then why didn't you tell someone?" I asked. I knew that girls told everything. They always did. They couldn't keep a secret for five minutes.

"Who'd believe me any more than they'd believe you? And besides, who said I wanted to tell? Who said I wasn't just as interested in keeping it all a secret as you?"

I felt my eyes open several degrees at hearing this statement. Then I closed them into suspicious slivers, a trick I'd learned earlier in the year when I was becoming a famous detective.

"You mean you actually aren't going to give it all away? You aren't going to tell anyone?"

Amelia jumped up and ran to the window. She stood there for a long time, looking out. Then she turned around suddenly, her curls flying out. Her eyes were flashing.

"No, I'm *not,* Rupert P-for-Peevely, which I've known about all my life and never told anybody,

Brown! Even if I could and anyone would believe me, I wouldn't. Who says I can't be just as interested in a witch as you? Just because I'm not a . . . not a . . . crazy scientist like you doesn't mean I can't be as interested as you. I don't know how you got to be friends with the witch side of Miss Switch. It wasn't during school, I know that. It must have been after school, maybe even at night when it's witching time. I suppose you could because you're a boy and you can go out on night adventures and I can't because I'm a girl. Oh, it just isn't fair!" Amelia threw herself down on the bed, put her head on her arms and began to sob.

I stood there. Then I stood there a little longer. I knew that girls cried all the time, but it really bothered me to see Amelia the snoop crying in *my* room over something *I'd* done.

"Heck, Amelia," I said, looking down at the floor and kicking one foot around, "I just didn't know."

"Well, you know now!" said a stern voice from my desk. It was Guinevere. "You boys, always going around with your noses buried in a book or a test tube, or a football game."

11

Rupert's Secret Solution

I rose from Amelia Daley's front porch steps, crawled under some large shrubs by the house, flicked on my flashlight, and looked at the watch on my wrist. Then I turned off the flashlight, crawled back out from the shrubs, and went back to sit on the bottom step of the porch. It was fifteen minutes before midnight on the Monday following the Saturday of the football game.

Girls! I remarked to myself. I was sure that Amelia would be at least a half hour late, and I'd promised Miss Switch when I saw her at recess that

I'd be at school on the stroke of twelve.

Miss Switch wouldn't tell me anything when I'd talked to her except that she wanted to see me that night. I could tell from the way she acted, though, that the news from the computowitch was bad.

I began to wish I hadn't told Amelia she could come with me. Things were bad enough without my having to explain Amelia's presence, especially if she was going to make us late. I had just decided that I'd probably better go off and leave her when the front door opened slowly and Amelia tiptoed out. "It's spooky!" she whispered.

"What did you expect at this hour?" I said, putting my flashlight under one arm and my hands in my pockets as if I'd been running around at midnight all my life.

"I guess I don't know. You must be pretty brave to have been out all alone before," Amelia said. I suddenly discovered how it felt to have my chest swell. "Anyway," she continued, "I've brought us something."

She handed me a small bag hanging from a string. "I've got one too. Here, put it around your neck the way I'm doing."

"What in heck is that?" I asked.

"It's a kind of charm. They used to wear them in the old days against evil spirits."

"I'm not going to wear anything silly like that. Miss Switch would laugh her head off. She doesn't believe in all those old superstitions."

"Don't get mad," Amelia said. "It's only a ginger cookie and some raisins. I thought we might get hungry."

"Oh, that's different," I said. "Anyway, come on, let's get going or we'll be late." I started running, and Amelia followed.

It was a dark night, with the moon hidden behind clouds. For some reason it seemed darker than ever before. Quieter than usual, too. I had to admit to myself that it was nice having Amelia along with me. When we reached the playground, I couldn't remember it being so big and frightening before. Amelia reached out for my hand. I didn't want to hurt her feelings or anything like that, so I didn't pull my hand away. Together we ran for the school building. I could see the dim light shining from the windows of Room Twenty, so I knew Miss Switch was there.

"Come on," I said to Amelia. "I'll hoist you up."

"No, I can get myself up. You go first. All of a sudden I'm scared."

"Look at it this way, Amelia," I said. "It's only Miss Switch. You sit and look at her all day and you're not scared."

"This is different. You know it is!"

"Oh, all right!" I said. I climbed up and through the window. Then I leaned over the sill and helped Amelia up. She didn't need much help, though.

Even though I'd looked at the scene in front of me before, it still made my mouth go dry and prickles run up the back of my neck when I saw it. I didn't blame Amelia for gasping.

"Oh, Rupert, just like a real witch!"

"Of course. What did you think?" I said, sounding annoyed. Actually, I was rather proud showing Miss Switch to Amelia, as if I'd invented her myself.

Miss Switch didn't seem to have heard us. She was sitting at her desk, her pointed chin resting on her hands, and she was gazing miserably into the Bunsen burner.

With no warning at all, she suddenly looked up. Her green eyes flicked from Amelia to me and back to Amelia again. Then she leaped up from her desk, leaned over it with her hands resting one on either side of the flickering blue flame. Her eyes flashed, shooting out sparks in all directions.

"What is *this?*" she shrieked.

"It's me," I said in a small voice. "And this is Amelia Daley."

"So I see! And who, may I ask, Rupert, gave you permission to bring a guest?"

Amelia stepped forward bravely. "It's all my fault, Miss Switch, really it is. I begged him to bring me. He didn't want to at first. I found out about your being a witch myself. Rupert didn't tell me, really he didn't. It was only after I told him all I knew that he told me the rest of it. Please don't be angry with him! I'm not going to tell on you. I wouldn't even if someone *did* believe me. I just want to be in on it all. Oh, please!"

I pushed Amelia aside. "Well, it's my fault, too, Miss Switch. I'm not going to let Amelia take all the blame."

"Oh rubbish!" Miss Switch said. "I'm not the least bit interested in whose fault it is." She stared right into Amelia's face, and I was proud to see Amelia staring right back. "Hmmmmmph!" Miss Switch snorted. "So you're here and you're here. Facts are facts. What's done can't be undone. And all those other popular sayings. The way things are going, I'm not sure that it really matters anymore. I suppose Rupert has told you what I'm doing here at Pepperdine?"

"Oh yes, about the computowitch and all of it. Oh, Miss Switch, did it come out all right? Please tell us!"

"Well, there's no use mincing words," Miss Switch said. She jumped up from her desk, picked up a piece of chalk at the blackboard, and wrote:

Originality of idea . . . . Excellent
Performance . . . . F
Overall mark . . . . .F

Then she swung around and said, "I don't suppose I need to explain what an F means?"

"I've never heard of them," I said.

Miss Switch gave me a nasty look. "Failure!" she snapped.

"Oh, Miss Switch! That's isn't fair!" Amelia cried out. Then, to my horror, she ran and threw her arms around Miss Switch, black cloak and all. I thought I'd faint. I don't think it's necessary to report that I wouldn't put my arms around a witch for one billion nine hundred ninety-nine thousand dollars. I wouldn't even put my arms around a grown lady unless it was my mother. But a witch! Amelia had lost her mind.

The funny part of it was that Miss Switch almost looked as if she liked it. I would suppose that she'd never had anyone do that before. It didn't last long, though. "Fair, fiddlesticks! Witchcraft is not concerned with fairness, Amelia. Let's have no further sentimental nonsense about it. Now, take a desk, each of you."

That command sounded rather comfortable and like school. Amelia and I glanced at each other, found our desks, and sat down.

"Take out pencil and paper, please," Miss Switch ordered.

Getting out pencil and paper meant one thing to me. "Heck, Miss Switch," I said, "what do we have to go and have a test for?"

"Don't be dense, Rupert!" Miss Switch snapped. "The pencil and paper are merely to help you think. The fact is I've asked for and been given a second chance by the Witches' Council."

Amelia clapped her hands, and I couldn't help shouting "Hurrah!"

"Hurrah, nothing!" Miss Switch growled. "If I fail this time, I may be sweeping that blasted mountain for the rest of my life."

The rest of your life sounded like a long time to have to sweep a mountain. One hundred and fifty years seemed bad enough. I considered the fact of my mother not being able to get me to sweep my room, which normally took me about ten seconds.

"Oh, Miss Switch!" Amelia breathed.

"Wow, that's terrible!" I said. "All things considered, I think I'd stick with the first offer, Miss Switch."

"The only thing I care to consider at this moment is ideas. Am I to understand that you've run out of them, Rupert?" Miss Switch moved toward me with a menacing look in her eyes.

"Oh no!" I said quickly. "But look, Miss Switch, are you sure you want my help? You didn't do very well the first time around with me."

"That is for me to decide," said Miss Switch. "Now, get to work!"

The room became hushed. Miss Switch sat down again at her desk and was once more resting her chin on her hands and staring into the Bunsen burner. Bathsheba sat near it, washing her tail. Amelia and I sat staring at our pieces of paper and chewing our pencils.

I raised my hand. It seemed the proper thing to do under the circumstances.

"Speak up!" said Miss Switch.

"How about some kind of magic potion to make everyone light as air—you know, floating around?" I suggested.

"If you mean a levitation trick, that's been done before. Why, there isn't a magic act around that doesn't do something of the sort. You'll have to do better than that, Rupert."

"How about making everyone heavy as lead?" I knew I was just grabbing at straws. Miss Switch let me know what she thought by giving me a nasty stare.

I went back to chewing my pencil eraser. In the quiet classroom with only the small, dim light burning in front, I found it difficult to keep my mind on what I was supposed to be doing. My thoughts began to wander away from ideas on original witchcraft toward what had been happening in that very classroom in the past months. And somehow I was thinking more about Miss Switch the teacher than Miss Switch the witch. I kept thinking and thinking and then . . .

"I've got it!" I cried.

Amelia dropped her pencil and it clattered to the floor. Bathsheba jumped and hissed with fright.

"Well, now that you've succeeded in scaring us to death, Rupert, what is it you have to say?"

"Miss Switch, would you consider taking me someplace on your broomstick on Halloween? That's next Saturday, you know."

Miss Switch stiffened. "I know when it is! But for your information, Rupert, this is a business meeting. We are not here to discuss broomstick rides for you on Halloween."

"But, Miss Switch, this *is* business, the business of saving you from a . . . a fate worse than death!"

"You don't have to get so dramatic, Rupert. I only hope that whatever the business is, it's more original that that remark. Come, out with it."

"I can't," I said firmly.

"What do you mean, you can't!" snorted Miss Switch. "You mean you *won't,* don't you?"

"You can put it any way you want to, Miss Switch, but this is something I have to write out personally in front of the Witches' Council and put in the computowitch myself. It concerns original witchcraft you've already performed, and that's all I'll say."

"Already performed!" Miss Switch exclaimed.

"Well, if I've already performed it, why don't *I* know about it?"

"I can't explain that," I said, and clamped my lips together.

Miss Switch's eyes narrowed suspiciously. "This isn't just a ruse for you to get a look at the computowitch, is it, Rupert?"

"I'll have to be honest, Miss Switch," I said. "That thought had crossed my mind. But you'll have to take my word for it, science has nothing to do with this. I happen to believe that the Witches' Council would never accept this information if you presented it yourself. I'm the only one who can."

"Are you asking me to stake my future on something I don't even know about? How do I know if this idea of yours is any good?"

"Miss Switch," I said, putting my hand over my heart, "I'll stake my scientific life on it!"

Miss Switch looked at me slyly from around the Bunsen burner. "The computowitch had better find it good, Rupert, or it might very well mean your life as well as my future."

I must confess that I hadn't intended to stake my scientific life *that* far, but I felt that I couldn't back out at this point.

"Miss Switch," I began hesitantly, "it's not my fault that you're in the mess you're in now. The idea you got Excellent on was mine, you know."

It was a bold thing to say when you consider I was still dealing with a witch. For a long time Miss Switch said nothing. She just sat rubbing her chin and staring into the Bunsen burner. Then I heard her muttering to Bathsheba.

"He's absolutely right, you know, cat. I was the one who bungled the job. And if it's, as he says, something I've already done, I won't have to worry about bungling again. Hmmmm, he did get an Excellent on his idea, after all. I see no reason to think he won't again with his fertile scientific brain. It's a risk, cat, but I think I'll take it. And as for going on Halloween, I don't know where he got that idea, but as it turns out, it's the night I was commanded to report my accomplishments anyway. But I won't tell *him* that. I'll make him think I'm doing him a favor."

I listened to all this with my ears quivering, and very nearly fell out of my desk when Miss Switch said, "Very well, Rupert! It shall be as you say. I see no reason why I can't oblige you by taking you to Witch's Mountain on Halloween. I can pick you up at your window at a quarter to midnight, if it suits you."

"But how about me?" Amelia asked.

She was sitting there so quietly I'd forgotten all about her.

"You'd be scared stiff riding around on a broomstick, Amelia," I told her.

Amelia stood up from her desk and stamped her foot. Her eyes flashed. "I would *not!*"

For some unknown reason, my head began to whirl. What was wrong? I asked myself. Was I being bewitched by Amelia?

Then I heard a strange voice coming from somewhere and saying, "Miss Switch, I think Amelia had better come along. I think I'm going to need her, you know, as a sort of precaution, like the . . . like the toadstools and bat wings." It was *my* voice!

Miss Switch smiled her broad, thin smile. "I'm glad to see you getting some *real* sense, Rupert. After all, in the matter of witchcraft, you can't be too careful!"

Rupert P. Brown III, scientist, now up to his ears in witchcraft, smiled weakly back.

12

Witch's Mountain

I was both excited and scared about my forthcoming journey, and came close to changing my mind at least five hundred eighty-three and one-half times before Halloween. Was saving Miss Switch the witch from a terrible fate worth risking my scientific life? After all, it was only sweeping a mountain I'd be saving her from, but what a loss to science if anything ever happened to me. I could hardly bear to think about it. Yet, when I thought of saving good old Miss Switch the teacher, I knew I had to go.

I must confess, though, to one other thing that

kept me from changing my mind. I hadn't lied to Miss Switch when I'd told her that I had to hand in the information at Witch's Mountain personally, but didn't I owe it to science to see and possibly examine the computowitch? It was entirely possible that I might be the only scientist in the whole world who ever would!

Of course, I must also add that, on the lighter side, I didn't want to give up a broomstick ride. How many fifth grade boys did I know, I asked myself, who'd been to Witch's Mountain on a broomstick? No, when it all boiled down to making a final decision, I knew that I wouldn't change my mind about going.

Halloween arrived at last. I didn't go anywhere that night, but just fooled around at home until bedtime. Then the hours until midnight really dragged. I lay under my bedcovers, completely dressed and stiff with excitement, waiting for a sign from Miss Switch. It came at last, something brushing against my window. It was the swishing sound of a broom brushing against glass. I leaped out of bed and tore to the window.

Looking out, I saw Miss Switch, all in black, hanging over our yard on her broom like an enormous night cloud. Bathsheba sat directly in front of Miss Switch, her cat's eyes shining through the darkness with the intensity of big green headlamps. I pulled off my glasses, wiped them on my trousers, and put them back on again. I wanted to get a perfectly clear view of this phenomenal picture.

"Okay, Miss Switch," I called out in a loud whisper. "I'm ready!"

She made a wide turn around the garden on her broom and sailed up close to the window. The broom hung there in midair. It was quivering slightly like a car with the engine running.

Suddenly Bathsheba let out a howl. Her tail fanned into a huge black bottle brush.

"What's that?" she snarled, peering into my room.

"What's what?" I said.

"That gold thing!"

"Oh, that's my saxophone," I explained.

Bathsheba turned and held a whispered conversation with Miss Switch.

"Bring it along," the cat said finally. "I'm tired of yowling alone on Halloween."

"But . . ." I began. As far as I knew, I wasn't going to Witch's Mountain to give a saxophone concert.

"Bring it along!" Miss Switch hissed. "You heard what the cat said. And hurry up about it. We haven't got all night!"

Miss Switch didn't sound very polite. She seemed to have forgotten that I was embarking on this dangerous mission to protect *her* future. Still, I didn't care to argue with her under the circumstances, so I hung my saxophone around my neck and climbed up on the windowsill. Then, with my heart pounding so hard I could hardly breathe, I climbed onto the broomstick. We glided off without a sound.

In less than thirty seconds we were at Amelia's house. She was already sitting on the windowsill waiting for us, dressed in . . . I nearly fell off the broomstick when I saw it! She was dressed in exactly the same kind of clothes as Miss Switch—a flowing black skirt and little black cape—and she wore a small, pointed black hat. Furthermore, her brown curls were gone. Hanging out from under her hat was long, dark, *straight* hair!

I was sure that in spite of what she'd said, she was going to be scared green and that I'd have to climb off the broom to help her on. Instead, she slid right on behind me as if she'd been riding around on a broomstick all her life. I turned around to look at her. In the moonlight her eyes were flashing with excitement.

"I'm on, Miss Switch!" she cried.

Miss Switch gave a wild, cackling laugh, and we soared off into the night.

I found myself forgetting where we were going and why. All I could think of at that moment was BROOMSTICK RIDE! Amelia and I were actually on a BROOMSTICK RIDE! I couldn't get over it.

A broomstick ride is something impossible for an ordinary scientist to describe. I even went so far then as to consider becoming a great poet when I returned, *if* I returned, so that I could describe the feeling of having night all around me as if I were a bird. To be able almost to touch it, to be able almost to touch the stars. And the wind, too! It seemed to be singing through our hair.

I think I wasn't the only one on that broomstick who seemed to have forgotten the desperate mission we were on. When I looked up at the moon and said, almost to myself, "It's funny, but with everybody going up there now, I guess the moon won't be mysterious anymore," Miss Switch shouted out happily, "Rubbish! The moon will always be mysterious, Rupert. Just as the world you live in will always be mysterious. I've been around long enough. I ought to know. Look at the moon now. It's like a globe of ice!"

"It looks more like a pale persimmon to me!" Amelia shouted.

"A golden orange!" I cried.

"Have it your own way!" shouted Miss Switch. "Hold on, we're going down."

"Are we going to land?" I asked.

"No, just having a little Halloween fun. We'll skim around a while and see what we can see."

"Watch out!" I shouted. "There's a line of laundry. We're going to run right into it!"

"No such thing!"

"It looks like birds flapping in the wind!" Amelia cried.

"Splendid!" screamed Miss Switch. "Now, just watch me!"

The broomstick rode even lower and, as it swooped across the laundry lines, Miss Switch reached out and undid the clothespins. I gasped as the laundry, instead of falling to the ground, flew off into the air. The shirts flapped their arms, and the trousers waved their legs, and they flew off like mammoth white birds. We watched them soaring and sailing up toward the moon.

"Where will they go?" I asked.

"Wherever birds—and laundry—go on Halloween. They'll be back by dawn. They always are."

"That was splendid, Miss Switch," I said.

"*I* thought so," she said.

We flew on and on.

"Oh, look at the apple trees below!" Amelia shouted. "I wonder what it would feel like to bob for an apple from a flying broom."

"We'll soon find out!" cried Miss Switch. She dipped the broom downward, and as she sailed over the trees, I reached out and picked a red apple. Then Amelia reached into another tree and picked a gold one.

Then Miss Switch herself reached down, but instead of picking an apple, she shook first one tree and then another. The leaves that were still left on the trees all fell to the ground, but all the apples flew off from the trees and drifted up into the air. They were like miniature red and gold balloons. We watched them sail away until they were all lost in the blinking stars.

On we sailed and drifted and blew with the

night wind. We could look down to where the windows of tall buildings twinkled like stars, and up to where the stars blinked like the windows of tall buildings.

And then, almost with no warning, there were no more stars and no tall buildings. The night grew very dark and very cold. The moon disappeared, and mist swirled around us.

I shivered and squeezed the broom handle harder. No one needed to tell me we were approaching the place where no human person had ever been before, the place where Miss Switch's whole future was at stake, not to mention my very own life—Witch's Mountain!

We flew on and on in the clammy mist. Miss Switch had become silent. There was no more Halloween fun. Amelia was quiet, too, and was now holding *me* instead of the broom handle. She didn't have to say anything. I knew that she knew.

Gradually the mist began to shimmer in a pale and ghostly way. I looked up and saw that the moon had reappeared, but it hardly gave any light. It just looked down at us like a cold, green eye of ice. Suddenly, directly ahead of us, a huge shadow rose through the mist, dark and silent and terrible.

This, I knew, was Witch's Mountain!

Miss Switch said nothing, but she directed the broomstick downward, circling around and around in huge, silent circles until at last we glided to a halt on the rocky, barren ground. The mist rose up around us and crept up over the mountain as we all got off the broomstick.

"Where do we go now, Miss Switch?" I asked, trying to hide the quaver in my voice.

"Sssssssss!" Miss Switch hissed at me. "Quiet!" She peered into the mist. "Bathsheba, wait here with them. I see that the Witches' Council has already assembled."

"Should I come with you, Miss Switch?" I asked. I hoped, for Amelia's sake, that I was sounding stalwart and brave.

"Sssssssss!" Miss Switch hissed again. "I'll have to speak to them first. They will either agree to seeing you . . . or they won't!" She strode off into the mist.

"I wonder what happens if they *won't?*" I groaned. "I don't even know what happens if they *will!*"

Amelia slipped her hand into mine. "It's going to be all right, Rupert!" she whispered. "You'll see. I think you're the bravest boy who ever lived!"

I didn't find it necessary to tell Amelia that I was also the most scared. Together we stood looking off into the shadows and the mist where the Witches' Council was meeting. Bathsheba sat beside us calmly washing her paws. She could afford to be calm, I said to myself. She had nine lives and not one of them was presently being threatened.

Hours seemed to pass, but I suppose it was no more than ten minutes before Miss Switch returned. "They've agreed to see you, Rupert." She stared at me for a minute and finally muttered, "I'm a fool! I must be bewitched! Follow me, Rupert."

She must be bewitched! I considered that a very funny remark. With my knees feeling soft as jelly, I followed her. Bathsheba ran ahead, but Amelia stayed behind to walk with me.

When we reached the foot of the mountain, Miss Switch stopped. "I have to stay here," she said. "You will please step up in front of the Council where the Head Witch will question you."

"Witches' Council? Where?"

"Here!"

I looked around and then nearly collapsed. I'd thought we had come to a large pile of black boulders lying at the foot of the mountain, but these were black boulders—with *eyes!* At least thirty pairs of slanted, glass-green eyes were all staring at me from the faces of thirty witches, all sitting on the ground with their black skirts spread all around them.

"Y-y-y-y-you mean I have to stand in front of all th-th-these . . . n-n-nice people?" I stammered.

"Sssssssss!" Miss Switch hissed, and pushed me ahead.

"What shall I do with my saxophone?" I asked. I was still wearing it hung around my neck.

"Keep it. You may need it!"

Supposing that she meant as a weapon, I didn't find that to be a very comfortable farewell message. Everything I'd had for breakfast, lunch, and dinner the day before seemed to be sitting in my throat. My head was spinning. Holding my saxophone tightly, as if for support, I somehow managed to walk up to the front. I was in for another shock, the worst yet.

What had looked like the biggest boulder of all sitting in front of all the others suddenly threw back its head and let out a wild, cackling shriek of laughter.

"So, this is the little man who is going to save

Miss Switch, is it?" She screamed with laughter again. "Well, come, come, little man, step forward so I can have a good look at you."

Something I didn't like one bit was being called "little man," but under those conditions, who was I to complain? I stepped forward.

"Ssssssss! That's close enough!" The Head Witch drew back with a snarl. I noticed that she eyed my saxophone suspiciously.

Actually, I thought I was close enough, too. She was without any doubt the ugliest specimen of witch I'd seen up until then. She looked as if she was made entirely of hooks—hooked nose, hooked chin, hooked all over. Black eyebrows bushed out over her slanty green eyes. Her skin was soft and smooth as the bark of a rotting tree stump, and about the same color. Next to this witch, Miss Switch looked like a beauty contest winner. She sat rubbing a huge, hairy, black wart on her chin, and *staring* at me.

"So, you're the little man who has staked his scientific life on this venture, eh?"

"I . . . I . . . I guess so," I said.

"What do you mean, you guess so? It's a little late to be guessing about anything now, isn't it?

Well, out with it! What is this glorious idea for pro-
tecting your precious Miss Switch?"

I didn't like the way she said "precious Miss
Switch." It made me boil, just enough to answer
her back. I rubbed my saxophone pointedly, as if it
had special magical properties, stared straight into
the Head Witch's eyes, and said calmly, "I don't
intend to tell you anything!"

"What!" she screamed, rising to her feet. "How
dare you defy me, you nasty little creature! You'd
better tell me what's in that blasted little brain of
yours, or else you'll regret it seriously. I w-a-r-n
you!"

"It's no use threatening me when I have *this*," I
said, waving my saxophone under the Head
Witch's nose. She drew back with her clawed hands
before her face. "I intend to put the information
into the computowitch myself. Furthermore, if anything happened to me, you'd never know what
splendid original witchcraft it was that Miss Switch
performed, since she doesn't even know it herself.
You'd just have to go on guessing what it was for the
rest of your life, which could be a very long time in
your case. It could drive you crazy!"

The Head Witch thought this over a moment

and then threw back her head once more and let out a wild, earsplitting, shrieking howl of rage. Then she stopped suddenly. Her eyelids dropped down over her eyes until they formed nasty green slivers. She started to rub her chin again and stare at me. I fingered my saxophone and stared back.

"Very well, little man!" she snarled. "Follow me!" She turned and strode off, and I stumbled along after her. Hearing a strange moaning, rustling sound behind me, I looked around and saw the whole Witches' Council sliding through the mist after us. Behind them came Miss Switch, Amelia, and Bathsheba.

13

The Computowitch

I didn't know whether to break out in tears or come down with a case of hysterical laughter when I saw it, but the computowitch was the craziest, most unscientific-looking contraption I'd ever seen in my life, even in pictures. Except for two things— one, that it rose to a peak topped with a round cooking-pot lid, and two, that it had twenty-five cone-capped stovepipes going out in all directions instead of only one—the computowitch looked like nothing more than a small, black, old-fashioned coal cooking stove! I don't know what I expected to find, but it certainly wasn't anything like that.

I could tell, though, that the Head Witch was proud of it—even afraid of it, the way she approached it so gingerly.

But I couldn't restrain myself. "*That's* the *computowitch?*" I croaked.

The Head Witch whirled on me. "What's wrong with it?"

I shrugged. "I don't know. It's okay, I guess. I didn't know they looked like that."

"Well, this one does!" she snarled.

"Oh," I said, deciding it was useless to carry the discussion further. "Well then, where do I get the card and how do I punch it?"

The Head Witch opened a little door at the side of the computowitch and pulled out a rectangular piece of cardboard and a stick that looked like it was made of charcoal. "Here's your card," she said. Then she added icily, "And you don't punch anything. You write—with this."

She handed me the stick. It *was* charcoal, I discovered. That was logical. The computowitch looked like a stove so it probably manufactured its own pencils. The card looked much too small, though, especially if I had to write on it.

"I'll need more cards," I announced.

"You'll what?"

"More *cards!*" I said firmly.

The Head Witch made a threatening move toward me as if she were going to hit me. I tried not to cringe, but just stood firm, fingering the keys on my saxophone and looking at her boldly.

Her eyes narrowed. "How many?" She reached into the computowitch again and pulled out three cards.

"More," I said.

Growling and snarling at me, she continued to reach in and pull out more cards.

"That'll be enough, thanks," I said at last. I was holding a stack of cards about a foot high. "Now, if you don't mind, I'd like to be left alone." I sat down on the ground, unhooked my saxophone, and placed it carefully and ominously by my side.

The Head Witch snarled at me and stepped back about six feet. It wasn't far enough for me, but I didn't want to push my luck, so I tried to ignore her while she stood there rubbing the wart on her chin and glaring at me.

The first thing I did was to examine the cards. They were all blank. There were no instructions of any kind, so I just started out by writing, "Dear computowitch."

Then I wrote.

And I wrote.

And I wrote, filling out one card after another.

And I never wrote one card about the kind of original witchcraft Miss Switch had performed as a *witch,* but only the kind she had performed as a *teacher*!

Now, I realize that some people may not think this is very exciting, or the kind of thing you'd stake your whole scientific life on, but I think you'll understand when I state, as I did to the computowitch, that this year, for the very first time in their lives, Peatmouse, Creampuff, and Banana liked their teacher.

"Why, Mr. Computowitch," I wrote, "it is a personal well-known fact to me that these boys all starting hating their teachers before they were even born. But would you believe that only last week they all agreed that if they *had* to have someone as their mother besides the original one they had, they wouldn't mind if it was someone like Miss

Switch? If that isn't a pretty original type of witch-craft, I'd like to know what is!"

Of course, I also mentioned to the computo-witch that the whole class liked Miss Switch, but it was the boys liking her that made the difference. And it wasn't just my friends, either. All the boys acted as if they were bewitched. Take Billy Swanson, for instance. Billy had not only stopped spitting spitballs around at everyone, he was actu-ally seen by Banana bringing flowers to Miss Switch from his mother's garden. Melvin Bothwick not only stopped tattletaling, but even came up to me and apologized for giving out information about my middle name. And as for Peatmouse, Creampuff, and Banana, well, they were working so hard for a change that on their report cards Creampuff didn't get a single D, Banana got a cou-ple of B's, and Peatmouse actually got one whole unqualified A. In English!

I didn't try to offer the computowitch any explanation of how this witchcraft had taken effect, but I did say that Miss Switch was the fairest teacher we'd ever had, even if she was the strictest. "Fair, fiddlesticks!" she'd said, but in the classroom she sure didn't act like she meant that. "Do you know, Mr. Computowitch," I wrote, "that Miss Switch doesn't even have a teacher's pet? That's pretty fair, if you ask me."

Well, anyway, that's the kind of stuff I wrote to the computowitch. I ended up by saying that in this day of scientific wonders, people going to the moon and beyond and all that, things like I'd suggested to Miss Switch—making people lighter than air or heavier than lead—weren't considered original anymore. Nothing much in witchcraft was, and that's why I felt it should seriously consider this idea. That was my closing remark.

When I'd really finished, every card was used up, and my charcoal was down to a stub. I was practically dead from exhaustion when I breathed out, "I'm finished!"

"Well, let me have the cards," the Head Witch ordered at once.

I quickly picked up my saxophone and hung it back around my neck. "I'll put them in the computowitch myself," I said. "Just tell me where to do it."

"Right in there," the Head Witch snorted, pointing to a small opening in the computowitch. "Press this button, then put them into the opening one at a time." Then she added slyly, "And I hope it's worth all your trouble, little man!" Needless to say, except for the "little man" part, those were my feelings exactly.

Before pressing the button, I looked around me. The rest of the Witches' Council had all moved in, pressing closely around the Head Witch. I was surrounded by a sea of slanting green eyes and expressionless white faces. I looked for Miss Switch, Amelia, and Bathsheba and finally saw them. Amelia began to smile and wave at me, but Miss Switch, standing beside her, quickly pulled her arm down.

I pressed the button and pushed in my first card. At first nothing much happened. Then the computowitch lit up with a pale green glow, and from down in its insides came a faint rumble-grumble as if it was having indigestion. I fed in a few more cards, and the green glow turned to pale pink. The noises grew a little louder. But it was when I put in the card where I'd mentioned about the boys considering a person like Miss Switch for their mother that everything began to break loose.

The pale pink changed to a brilliant, fearsome red. The rumbling noises became a fierce roar.

Gusts of smoke began to pour out of all the capped stovepipes.

"Has it ever acted this way before?" I asked, directing my question to the Head Witch.

"Never!"

"Should I go on?"

"It's your funeral," she replied cheerfully.

I looked desperately over toward Miss Switch. She gave me a slight nod, and it was all I needed. I began feeding in more cards.

Louder and wilder, the colors inside it going like a kaleidoscope, the computowitch changed violently from red to orange to purple and back to red again, roaring and raging and pumping out smoky blasts. When I put in the card about Peatmouse getting an A in English, its sides actually began to heave in and out, and it started to dance madly about on its curved black feet.

I fed in card after card after card. The computowitch went completely berserk, churning and roaring and bellowing, pouring out smoke and sparks. It looked as if it would burst its seams and explode, but I continued to leap around, keeping out of its way and still feeding in cards until the very last one had been pushed through.

Then suddenly, just as the last card disappeared through the opening, the noises ended, the lights went out, and the computowitch stopped dead. Nothing was left of all the activity but a few wreaths of smoke floating over its cooking-pot lid.

Had the miserable machine conked out just as it was about to report on Miss Switch? I asked myself. Without thinking, I did what I often do to our television set at home, I reached out and gave the computowitch a big slap on its lid. The computowitch just sat there doing nothing for a moment, then it heaved one tremendous, shuddering sigh and squeezed a single card through its opening. I quickly made a grab for it.

It was the last card I'd written about Miss Switch, and across the face of it were two words printed in large, smudged charcoal letters. "EXCELLENT! PASSED!" I screamed out.

I suppose I expected a great roar of approval to rise up from the Witches' Council. Instead, my cry was greeted with deadly silence. It didn't take much thought to realize why. They were all wondering what happened to their computowitch.

Frantically I turned and began punching the "go" button and any other button I could find on it. I shook it, kicked it, and banged on it. But nothing happened. It just sat there looking dark and dismal—and wrecked! My scientific experience hadn't gone much beyond moldy oranges, nutritional experiments, and a few items such as burning holes in my blanket with my magnifying glass. I had to admit it. I was no computer repair expert.

There was nothing more I could do, so I turned to face the Witches' Council and said, "I'm afraid I've busted your machine." As final remarks go, it wasn't very outstanding.

Then, not wanting to watch myself being torn to ribbons by a lot of angry witches, I closed my eyes and waited. I waited and waited and I waited. Finally I got tired of waiting and opened my eyes again.

The witches were still standing in the same place, staring at me and the computowitch. No one had moved one inch toward me. At that moment I noticed a very unusual thing. The thin black lines that were the witches' mouths were all turning upward, and I realized with a jolt that the witches were actually smiling. Then it came back to me how much Miss Switch had hated the computowitch. They all hate it, I told myself in amazement.

Except for Miss Switch, it had passed them all once, but how about the next time, and the next? They might not be so lucky. They were *glad* that I'd wrecked it!

But how about the Head Witch? How did she feel about it? I watched her anxiously.

She approached the computowitch and poked it cautiously with a long, bony finger. "Are you absolutely sure it's—*busted?*"

"It is as far as I'm concerned," I said truthfully.

"Hmmmm," she said, rubbing her wart. "And you're quite sure it can't be fixed?"

"Well, all I know is, *I* can't fix it," I said.

The Head Witch glared suspiciously around at the rest of the Council. "Is there anyone here who *can?*"

The witches all looked at each other and shook their heads. Except one. One tall black shadow separated itself from the rest and slunk off into the mist. I suspected that that was the witch who'd suggested the computowitch in the first place. I wouldn't have wanted to be in her shoes when this was all over, I thought.

"In that case," said the Head Witch, rubbing her hands together gleefully, "I officially declare the computowitch permanently out of order. It shall henceforth be used as a . . . as a . . ."

"Stove?" I suggested.

"Stove! Splendid, my good man!"

I noticed that I'd graduated from "little man" to "good man." It was a nice promotion.

A murmur of approval greeted the Head Witch's announcement as the witches all turned to each other and nodded. The Head Witch then leaned over the computowitch, lifted up its cooking-pot lid, and peered in. A crafty look spread over her face. "Yes," she said, "*quite* busted!"

Then she drew back one leg and with her pointed boot gave the computowitch a magnificent, shuddering kick right in it ornamented middle. "Take that, you miserable machine! We can be perfectly acceptable witches without your blasted help!"

And with that final kick from the Head Witch, all the cards I'd written came floating out of the computowitch. "Aha!" she said, pouncing on them. "Now let's see what this splendid bit of mischief is that did you in."

She began to read them aloud while I stood to one side trying to look modest as she said from time to time, "Hmmmm, excellent! Original witchcraft indeed!" And then when she'd ended, she said, "Well, we must certainly keep this information. After all, you can never tell when we might be able to use some of this again—eh?" She gave me a crafty, confidential smile. "In the meantime, I shall entrust them to the charge of . . . Miss Switch!"

"Oh boy!" I shouted. "I'll take them to her."

"Oh no you won't!" snarled the Head Witch. Now what? I asked myself.

"You aren't going anyplace until you explain *that!*" She shuddered and pointed to my saxophone.

"Oh, it's a rather rare kind of magical charm," I said with an official shrug. "It's called a saxophone." Without thinking, I put my lips to it and blew. Out came one of my usual sour, ear-splitting notes, the kind Caruso had mentioned. I stopped immediately.

For a few moments the Head Witch stared off into space as if she'd gone into a trance. Then, "Do that again!" she commanded.

"You're kidding!" I said.

Bathsheba bounced over to me. "Play! Play!" she hissed. "Don't you know it's the most beautiful music she's ever heard?"

So I put my saxophone to my lips again and

128

began to play. Every note was just as sour and horrible as the last, but when they heard them, all the witches began to dip and sway, their black skirts billowing out in the mist.

"It's the ancient dance of the witches," Bathsheba said.

Miss Switch was dancing with them. And even Amelia joined in.

Did I ever feel like something special! I'd saved Miss Switch. I'd made everybody happy by busting the computowitch. And I was even providing dance music.

What a hero!

14

Rupert P. Brown III, Scientist, on the Trail Again

Monday morning I came down with a cold. Amelia arrived that afternoon with a small package from Miss Switch.

"What's this?" I asked, turning it over in my hands.

"Henbane," said Amelia.

"But that's poison!"

"Of course it's poison," Amelia said. "Miss Switch didn't say to *take* it, silly. She just said to put it on your windowsill tonight. It'll cure your cold."

"Did she say anything else? I mean, about my

saving her, and the computowitch getting busted and all that?"

The witches' dance had lasted until the early hours of the morning and we had to race to get home before dawn. I'd been so tired I almost fell off the broomstick, and Miss Switch had hardly said anything. She didn't even thank me for rescuing her. I didn't mind, though. I thought she would probably do that back at Pepperdine the first chance she got.

A strange look crept into Amelia's eyes. "No, she didn't. She didn't say anything. I think something's wrong, Rupert."

"Oh no!" I groaned. "Do I have to rescue her again?"

"I don't know. I just wish you'd get over your cold and get back to school."

Well, something was wrong, all right. I found out what it was the day I got back to school. That was three days later. The henbane hadn't worked too well, and I'd made a mental note to mention it to Miss Switch that it had a musty odor about it. I never got around to saying it, though, because the afternoon of the day I returned to my fifth grade at Pepperdine, Miss Switch announced to the class that she was leaving.

Everyone was stunned.

"Oh no!" You could hear almost the whole class breathing the words.

"Oh, you can't!"

"Oh, you wouldn't!"

"I think I'm going to cry!" The person who said this was a girl.

Some of the girls actually did begin to cry. Everyone looked as if they wanted to. Even the boys.

As for me, I wanted to get up and shout, "You can't do that, Miss Switch! I didn't risk my whole scientific life just so you'd end up not being our teacher anymore. You wouldn't dare leave!" But I didn't get up and shout anything. I couldn't mess things up for Miss Switch, and I knew it probably wouldn't make much sense anyhow.

"Fiddlesticks and rubbish!" Miss Switch said sharply. "I haven't time for tears and foolishness. You'll have another teacher tomorrow and will soon forget all about me. Now pick up your books and hurry along, boys and girls. I have work to do."

Sniffling noisily, everyone filed out except Amelia and me. We hung around the classroom, and when the last person had left, Amelia burst out, "Oh, Miss Switch, it isn't fair!"

"You should have told us," I said. "I might not have . . . I might not have . . . well, risked my whole life if I'd thought it would mean you had to leave us. Amelia's right, it *isn't* fair!"

"Fair, fiddlesticks!" said Miss Switch. "After all, Rupert, I did wait until you returned to the classroom before leaving. And the matter of leaving or not was never part of the arrangement. I'm quite sure you would have offered to assist in helping me out no matter what the conditions."

"You're right, Miss Switch," I said. "But, heck, why do you have to go? You *have* to give us a reason."

"I have to do no such thing, Rupert. I'm simply returning full time to the other and first side of my nature. There's nothing more to be said."

"Oh, Miss Switch!" Amelia cried. "Don't you like it here? Don't you like being our teacher? You heard all those things Rupert wrote on the cards. You know how much the class likes you!"

"Well, that sentimental nonsense is *their* business, Amelia. I'm simply not interested in how much anyone likes me. A witch is a witch is a witch. That can't be changed."

"Won't . . . won't we ever see you again, Miss Switch?" I asked.

"I expect not. Now, run along, children. I still have work to do." Miss Switch began to shuffle papers all over her desk. I could tell, though, that all she was doing was just shuffling. There was a strange look in her eyes. At last she got up and walked to the window.

"Oh, all right, then," she said in a gruff voice. "Sometimes when the moon is full and the night is clear, you might see a single cloud pass overhead."

"Is that all?" I asked.

"That's all."

"Would . . . would that cloud be you, Miss Switch?" I could barely hear Amelia, she was asking it so softly.

"I won't say it could be. But I won't say it couldn't be, either. Now, do run along!"

We turned and started slowly for the door.

"Rupert!"

Amelia and I both looked around. Miss Switch still had her back to us.

"Yes, Miss Switch?" I said.

"Rupert, please don't slouch! And Amelia . . ."

"Yes, Miss Switch?"

"Amelia, do pull your skirt down and tuck in your blouse. Won't you children *ever* learn?"

Miss Switch's back looked strange. The same kind of strange her eyes had looked. And it was also the same kind of strange my mother's back looks often when she's trying not to laugh—or cry.

"Good-bye, Miss Switch," Amelia said.

"And . . . thank you," I said.

Then we walked out of Room Twenty and out of the school.

It was Saturday. The snow was falling softly. It had started to fall early in the morning and had already covered my windowsill with a deep, white blanket. I'd watched the snow fall all through the breakfast hour when I sat at the table not eating anything. *Really* not eating anything. I was not hungry. *Really* not hungry. My mother suggested that she ought to call the doctor, and my father actually agreed. I told them not to bother, that I didn't have a problem a doctor could solve. Then I left the table so I wouldn't have to explain the problem. How could I?

How could I ever explain that I was finding it impossible to go back to my dull, ordinary life after all that had happened to me during the past couple of months? I went up to my room, flopped on the bed, and sat staring dismally out the window. How could I go back to being a simple, ordinary, fifth grade scientist and worrying about mildewed oranges and snails in an aquarium after dabbling about in witchcraft, *real* witchcraft? How could I go back to the classroom at Pepperdine and face having an ordinary teacher to teach us after Miss Switch?

I looked over at my live experiments. Caruso was just swimming around in his bowl. I would have given anything just to hear one more good aria, but all he did was poke his little green head out of the water like a wet pebble and stare at me once in a while. I was still trying to respect Hector and Guinevere's wishes about their guinea pig feed, so Hector spent most of his time with his nose in his bowl, while Guinevere just waddled around and looked at me with her bright, shoe-button eyes. Not one of the three had said a word since the afternoon Miss Switch had said good-bye to us.

Had they ever talked to me at all? I asked myself. I didn't remember it happening, but wasn't it possible that I might have fallen on my head, perhaps the night I went to explore my classroom at

Pepperdine, and then imagined all the rest of it—that Miss Switch was a witch, that Amelia and I had gone with her to Witch's Mountain on a broomstick, and that I'd messed around with something called a computowitch? computowitch! I *must* have imagined a crazy thing like that. For that matter, I must have imagined the crazy thing I thought I'd seen the night before. I picked up my notebook and read the following aloud:

What: Cloud
Kind: Cumulus in the form of Miss Switch
Whose: The sky's
Performance: Waved at me
How Tested: No known way to prove scientifically

"Oh baloney!" I said, slamming the notebook shut. "Who'd ever believe any of this stuff? I certainly don't!"

"Well, I *do!*" a voice said from the doorway.

It was Amelia standing there with snowflakes all over her hair. She ran in and threw her coat on the bed.

"Oh, Rupert, did you really see her? Did you?"

"Heck, Amelia, I don't know. I don't know anything right now. All I do know is that I'm beginning to think I was right in the first place—if you can't prove it scientifically, it didn't happen. As for seeing Miss Switch in the sky, phooey! I think maybe I ought to go and get my glasses checked!"

"Rupert P. Brown III, you sound just like . . . *parents!* I suppose you think that Miss Switch wasn't even a witch, or that we never went with her on a broomstick to Witch's Mountain, or that you never saw a computowitch. Well, in case you've forgotten, I was in on all of it, too, and should be all the proof you need. You don't need to prove *everything* in a test tube. Would you like to know something, Rupert P. Brown III? There are smart scientists and there are dumb scientists, and you are a very dumb scientist. Well, you don't have to prove to *me* that you saw Miss Switch in the sky. *I* believe you did. And someday I expect to see her too. So there!"

"Gosh, Amelia," I said, "I don't think that . . ."

"Fiddlesticks!" said Amelia.

"I mean, I don't see how . . ."

"Poppycock!" Amelia folded her arms and glared at me. For a moment I almost thought I saw sparks shooting out of her eyes.

Suddenly my appetite came back with a blast.

Boy, was I starved! "Come on," I said, "let's go to the kitchen and see what we can find to eat."

Amelia raised her nose in the air. "Shall we take the broom, or do we have to go on foot?"

"On foot," I said. "The broom happens to be in the garage for repairs."

"Blast and botheration!" Amelia said. "But after we eat, could I look at some of your rock specimens through your microscope? You know, I'm thinking of starting a rock collection myself."

"No kidding!" I said. Well, I mean who ever heard of a fifth grade *girl* doing anything interesting like starting a rock collection?

It was then something struck me that I hadn't noticed before. Amelia wasn't wearing her hair in curls anymore. It was long and straight, the way she wore it the night we went to Witch's Mountain, the night she wore the black skirt and cape and tall, pointed hat, the night she danced with the witches, looking somewhat like a small witch herself.

My head began to spin and I felt a little dizzy as I thought this all through. And that was when I decided to start keeping another notebook.

My first entry reads like this:

What: Girl
Kind: Not certain
Whose: Mr. and Mrs. Daley's
Performance: Looked at rock specimens through
    microscope with *unusual* interest
How Tested: No known way to prove scientifically

After all, even though I've known Amelia all my life and don't suggest that she's a *witch* or anything like that, still, a girl is a girl is a girl—and I don't believe you can be too careful about anything.